D1028331

The Melbourne Connection

The

Melbourne

Connection

Joanne

Fisher

ACKNOWLEGEMENTS

Published by Joanne's Books www.joannesbooks.com

Published in the United States of America, 2021

ISBN: 978-1-0879-7338-8

Book Cover by: Macred Designs:

https://www.robin-mcdonald.com/home.html

Edited by Daniel B. Fisher

Cover Model: John Antorino, Actor, Model, Public Figure: Explore Talent Acting Profile - John Antorino

Dedication

I am dedicating this book to my dear friend of twenty years, from Canada, who passed away during the writing of this book, Theresa D'Iorio. TD, you will be sorely missed. Just know that you will always be close to my heart and in my prayers. Love you, girl! And keep on dancing in heaven!

The Melbourne Connection

Other Books by Joanne Fisher

With All of Me

With All of Me II

Her Spanish Doll

Good Things Always Happen in Springtime

Baker's Dozen Anthology

The Devil of St. Gabriel

Magnolia Blossom

The Melbourne Connection

Christmas in Venice

Christmas in Florence

Christmas in Rome

Traveling Boomers – First Stop Italy

Traveling Boomers – Second Stop Israel

The Melbourne Connection

Chapter 1

Melbourne, Australia

"Shut up!" Jack backhanded his wife, knocking her off her feet.

"B-but what did I do?" Fausta rubbed her cheek.

"Just shut the fuck up! I can't stand looking at you!" He threw the remote at her and stormed off down the hall.

Fausta couldn't cry anymore. She had no tears left. She was numb. All she wanted was to leave this brutal man. She gathered the pieces of the remote and put it back together again, like she had done dozens of times before. She placed the remote on the lamp table next to his favorite spot on the couch and went to the kitchen to prepare dinner. It was getting harder and harder to remember the good times they had before they got married.

~~~~~~

"Hey, what's your name?" Giacomo stepped in front of Fausta as she made her way to the science lab.

"Fausta," she shyly replied.

"Wow! That's a pretty name. Are you Italian?"

"Yes, my parents are. I was born in Melbourne, at the Francis Perry House."

"Really? What a coincidence. That's where I was born too! I guess that's where Italians like to have their babies." He raised an eyebrow and smiled. He ran his hand through the rebellious, almost-black hair that hung across his emerald-green eyes.

"I guess." Boy was he cute. She was mesmerized by him. So were the rest of the girls in school.

A shy beauty with chestnut hair, chocolate brown eyes and a pair of lips to die for, Fausta had the typical Italian olive complexion and, at only sixteen, the figure of a famous Italian actress like Gina Lollobrigida or Sofia Loren. As much as she tried to hide her full bosoms and her slim waist, the boys seemed to be noticing them more and more each day.

"You're really beautiful you know." Giacomo moved closer and softly ran his finger down the side of her face.

A shiver slithered down her spine. She'd heard around school how much of a charming Don Giovanni he was, so she'd been steering away from him since grade seven. But, still, she hoped he would notice her sooner or later.

"Ah, you say that to all the girls." She side stepped him and began walking.

He grabbed her arm. Her books flew out of her arms. "What did you do that for?" Irritated, she crouched to pick them up.

"No, let me." Giacomo quickly gathered all her books and handed them to her. "I'm sorry, I don't know what came over me."

She waited a few seconds to respond. "It's okay, but I have to leave now." This time he didn't stop her.

"Will I see you again?"

"Well, we do go to the same school so…yes." She blushed and smiled before disappearing into the classroom.

~~~~~~

They became inseparable. As soon as they finished high school, Jack proposed. By that time, he had already become a part of her family and she of his.

Both families were joyous at the news of their engagement even though Giacomo didn't have any job prospects.

"I will, but promise me that I can continue my studies." She asked her father.

"Why do you need to study? You need to stay home and raise your kids, just like your mother did. Giacomo will be the head of the family. He needs to work and support you and his family."

Fausta didn't argue with her father. She made her own plans instead. Once she was married, she could do whatever she wanted. She didn't need their parents' permission to go to college. "I'm going to make something of myself, if it's the last thing I do."

But when she told Jack of her plans, he didn't react as she had expected.

"No wife of mine will be working."

"But Jack, I want to help contribute."

Sometime during high school, Giacomo had morphed into Jack.

His green eyes flashed with anger.

"Are you mad?" She was afraid of the anger in his eyes.

He took a deep breath, smiled and said: "We'll see, okay? I'm not promising anything."

Feeling very encouraged, she hugged her fiancé. *I know I'll be able to convince him.* But as the engagement went on, that angry side of him came out more often. It gave her an uneasy feeling.

~~~~~~

West Melbourne wasn't the best part of town to live in, but the rents were the lowest there. On one income, that was all they could afford. Besides, it was a choice between living with her parents or living with his, and there was no way she was going to do that. She wanted to make her own way in life with Jack. It would be easier to convince him to let her continue her studies if they lived alone and with nobody to interfere.

On a rainy, dreary day in July of 1993, they wed. The dark clouds were much similar to the clouds in her heart. She almost changed her mind, but her bridesmaids and her mom kept her in line so to keep her mind off having cold feet.

The wedding was fancy and large and completely paid for by both parents. As per tradition, all the gift money went to the newlyweds so one day they could put a down payment on a house. They collected about twenty-five thousand dollars between the money gifts and the other gifts. They took a bit of that and went to Mount Martha beach for a short honeymoon. Jack had to come back and start his construction job that had been prepared for him by his father.

~~~~~~

One morning, while Jack was at work, she went to the bank and deposited the rest of the money in a savings account. She wanted to use it to study if Jack would let her. Her gut told her to not let her husband get his hands on it.

"Hey Carly, over here!" Fausta waved at her friend from the back of Sonny's Espresso Café. Carly McIntyre was her next-door neighbor growing up and her best friend since kindergarten. She had copper freckles and eyes that looked like clovers. She did everything she could to force her wild red hair straight but was unsuccessful. Instead, she upheld the fire-red curls that hung down to the crack of her behind either in a ponytail or with a clip.

Carly had always been on the plump side with a flat chest whereas Fausta was perfectly shaped. Carly would always say that she was supposed to be skinny and Fausta should have been plump because of Gabriella's wonderful cooking. "But no, we have to be the opposite, don't we?"

"Oh, hey girl." Carly plopped down and placed her shopping bags next to her. "Oh, smells divine in here."

The retro coffee shop was decorated with an authentic jute box in the back corner and a bunch of small tables along the side wall. On the other side there was two baristas who scurried to prepare the orders, a huge espresso machine, and the big blackboard with white chalk writing on it. It was updated daily with the special fresh baked goods that they received every morning.

"So, what are you having?"

Carly inspected the sweets display. "I'd like that one please and a cappuccino." Then she looked over to Fausta, "What are you having?"

"A chocolate chip scone and a latte with double shot of espresso." Her stomach growled with that order.

"You heard the lady." Carly waited in front of the cash register and paid the bill.

"You didn't have to do that."

"Oh, you can get it next time."

"Fine." She pouted.

"So, tell me, what did you do that brought you here?" Carly sat back and took a breath.

"Well, I deposited our gift money in a bank close by, and when I saw this espresso bar, I thought I'd text you."

"Well, I'm glad you did." Carly grabbed Fausta's hands. "So, tell me, how's married life."

"It's okay, I guess." She didn't sound enthusiastic.

"Okay? Come on Faussy, it's got to be better than okay."

Fausta smiled. Carly nicknamed her Faussy in middle school. Carly claimed it suited her because it rhymed with Sassy. "Well, I've noticed that he loves to drink." Her smile turned to a frown.

"Yeah, and?"

"He gets a bit violent."

"Violent? Oh, that's not good." Carly hesitated. "You'd better nip it in the bud, girl."

"How do I do that?"

"Stand up to him."

Fausta hesitated. "I'll try." Easier said than done.

"Good girl."

Their order arrived and Carly took a huge bite of her Danish and sipped her cappuccino. "Mmmmm, this is delicious!"

"Sure is."

"So, did you put his name on the savings account?"

"No, just mine."

"Smart girl. This way, if you need to get away, you have some back up."

"Get away? Oh, I would never leave Jack."

"Never say never." Carly took another large bite of her Danish.

"Yes, better safe than sorry."

~~~~~~

As soon as she got home, Fausta prepared dinner and had it hot and ready when Jack arrived.

"Smells great in here."

"Thanks honey." She so loved these moments.

After dinner, he asked: "Where did you put the money we made from our wedding?"

"In a savings account, of course." She smiled hoping for a positive reaction.

"Makes sense." He didn't ask for more details. He got up, grabbed a beer and headed to watch television.

Whew! She washed the dishes and cleaned up the kitchen as quietly as she could. Jack didn't like a lot of noise while he watched the TV.

The more Jack drank, the more his actions turned into physical and verbal abuse. She was so ashamed that she stopped having coffee with Carly. Many times, Fausta left the apartment to go back to her parents, but they weren't having any of it.

"You're on your own, Fausta. This is what married life is. You've got to play the cards you are dealt." Her father used a card reference since he loved to play cards.

"Your father is right, my daughter, you must stay with Giacomo. You'll see, things will get better."

It was hopeless. Both her parents were wrong. Two years had gone by. Was marriage supposed to be like this? For the umpteenth time she picked up her small bag and returned home to Jack.

Since, she didn't know who to turn to, she rekindled her friendship with her best friend. Carly had not married out of high school; she'd gone to college and got an Engineering degree. She was a single, working woman and enjoying every minute of it. She dated here and there but marriage was never on her mind. Her ultimate dream was to leave Australia and go to the US to work for NASA.

"One day, Faussy, one day!"

She loved Carly very much, but she was ashamed to tell her about Jack's abuse until one day, she popped over for tea and noticed the bruises on her face and arms.

"Are you kidding me?"

"It's not what you think?"

"Oh, it isn't? Then what is this?" pulling her arm to show the huge bruise. "And this?" she pulled her to her bedroom so she could look at herself. "Look! Look at what he's done to you!"

Fausta broke down and cried. "I can't lie to you Carly. I can't lie. I'm sorry." She blubbered and hung her head between her hands.

Carly sat down and pulled Fausta into her arms.

"Ow."

"Sorry, girlfriend. I'm trying not to squeeze too tight. Damn those bruises. And damn him anyway. It's okay, I'm your friend. I won't tell anyone. I promise." She pulled away. "But you can't live like this. This is wrong. Do you understand that?"

Sniffling, Fausta nodded. "I don't know how to make him stop. He gets angry at the smallest thing. It's like I flip some kind of switch in him. I don't know what to do."

"Let's make a pact."

Fausta nodded.

"Next time he touches you, you're coming to stay with me."

"Oh, I couldn't possibly place this burden on you. No way."

"Listen to me, Faussy, I don't care! Do you hear me? You're like the sister I never had, and I will NOT let that man abuse you. I will NOT!"

"I don't know what to do." Fausta dried her eyes with a tissue.

"Well...pack a small bag that you can grab on the fly."

"Okay."

"Put your savings booklet in there along with your jewelry, and keep it tucked away."

"Okay."

"And I want you to open another savings account, put about fifty dollars in it and make it available for him."

"Why do that?"

"I saw a movie about an abused wife who did what I'm suggesting. She was saved in the end. I know it's a movie, but it was based on a true story."

Fausta nodded. "All right. Can't hurt I guess."

"Good girl." Carly kissed her friend on the cheek. "The next time he beats you, you wait until he's fast asleep, and get the hell out of there!"

Fausta nodded. She was afraid that Jack would know where she went. She was afraid he would beat Carly too. "What if he finds me? Finds us?"

"You let me worry about that."

But when she went home, she did as she was told.

~~~~~~

Jack behaved himself for a good while. He would still get upset at the tiniest thing, but he hadn't laid a hand on her for several weeks. Until now, and his timing was terrible. She had some news that she knew in her heart would make him stop being how he was.

"Where is it?"

"Where is what honey?" she asked not looking him in the eye.

"The money!"

"Money?" She knew exactly what he was referring to.

"Stop! Just stop!" He backhanded her. She landed on her bum on the coffee table, shattering the glass.

She was cut and bleeding in a few places, but she didn't cry. She never cried no matter how much he beat her. Perhaps if she did, he would have pity on her and would stop. "I'm sorry Jack, I'm sorry, I don't know what money you're looking for." Slowly and quietly crying, she tried to get up and sit on the couch.

"Shut the fuck up! You know exactly what money I'm looking for. It's the savings money. Where is it?" He headed towards her with his hand raised. He'd smack her if she didn't give up the goods.

"In the bank. I told you years ago, I placed the money in a savings account." She covered her face with both forearms.

"All right then, where's the booklet?"

She got up. "I'll go get it." She stood right in front of him, lip bleeding, but held her head high. "Then, I have some news." She smiled.

"Yeah, yeah…go get the booklet." He pushed her towards the bedroom while he headed for the fridge to grab his fourth beer of the night.

When she entered the bedroom, she heard the beer tab being flipped open. "Crap, another beer." She whispered to herself. "This cannot be good." She went to the top dresser drawer and pulled out a savings booklet. It wasn't the original. "You called it Carly." She looked at the booklet that was a picture-perfect copy of the original that was stashed away in her emergency bag. She slid the drawer closed and headed for the living room. "Here you go Jack." She gave the booklet to him.

"Finally!" He grabbed it from her, looked it over, and shoved it in his shirt pocket. "I will take care of this baby from now on."

She didn't say a word. She went to the kitchen to put on a pair of cleaning gloves, then she went to the coffee table and started picking up hundreds of pieces of glass. She looked at Jack. He had a smirk on his face while he patted the booklet with his right hand and surfed the channels with his left.

It was that moment that she decided to call it quits. But how? How could Carly possibly get her out of this messy marriage?

The next morning, around seven, Carly dialed her best friend. She had news and she wanted to tell Fausta first.

"Hello?"

"Faussy, I've got news!"

She could hear the excitement in her friend's voice. "Oh, really, so do I." But Fausta wasn't as enthusiastic as Carly.

"That's wonderful! So, how about we meet at our usual place. I've got to pick up coffee before I head to work, so we can chat."

"All right, I'll be there in twenty."

"Bye then."

Fausta wondered what the news was as she wandered into their favorite coffee shop. Nobody knew about their secret meeting place, only the two of them. Fausta headed over to the counter. "Cappuccino please." She ordered as she picked up a tray and slid it down the line. When she pulled out her wallet to pay, Carly popped right in front of her and gave the cashier a twenty.

"My treat." She gave her friend a huge smile.

"Thanks Carly, but you didn't have to, really."

"Yes, I did."

They headed to their favorite table, but it was occupied.

"Let's go there. It's more private." Fausta pointed to a dark table in the back.

Carly raised an eyebrow. "Why back there? What's going on?"

As they made themselves comfortable, a very young and handsome waiter brought them their orders. "Here you go ladies." He winked and left.

"Cute huh? Gosh I'm in a great mood today. How are you? Not so good by the look on your face. Okay, spill it. Did he touch you again?"

Fausta nodded.

"That bastard! I swear I'm going to…"

"No, you're not going to do anything. I'm packed up. I'm leaving him for good now."

"Good! Finally. But why the sad face?"

Fausta took a deep breath. "I'm pregnant."

Carly gasped. "Pregnant? Does he know?"

"No. I was going to tell him but then he became violent and asked for the savings booklet."

"Okay, and you gave him the fake one, right?"

"I switched it out while he was sleeping."

"Good girl."

"Well, now what? I can't stay because if he finds out what I did, he'll kill me for sure."

Carly pressed her lips together. "Come with me."

"With you? Why, where are you going?"

A huge bright smile came across Carly's lips. "Remember my dream?"

"Of course, I remember your dream. You've only mentioned it a gazillion times."

"Right, well, I got a job offer from a company in the US that works in partnership with NASA. It's called RGF Space Solutions." She fainted a smile searching for Fausta's reaction.

"Oh my God, Carly, that's wonderful news! I'm so happy for you! I'll miss you, so much."

"No, you won't 'cause you're coming with me."

"With you?"

"Yes, what, are you deaf? Yes, with me. You can't stay here. It's too dangerous for you now."

"Indeed, it is. But I can't just leave the country. I won't know what to do with myself."

"We'll figure it out, come on, be bold."

"What about my mom…and dad?"

Carly crossed her arms. "What about them? They never supported you, and they never backed you up. They always sent you back to Jack. You have to cut ties now."

"I don't know if I can impose."

"Let me ask you then; do your parents know?"

"No, they don't."

"Good. Then don't tell them and leave with me."

"When?"

"They're flying me over for training, and they are going to pay for my move. It's all set."

"Are you sure about this?"

"Absolutely. Listen, you've got to leave now otherwise, if he finds out that you've taken his money and his kid, he will kill you and I won't be able to live with myself if he did. Please, Faussy, please come with me."

Fausta glared at her friend. Then she took a deep breath. "Right, okay, let's do this."

Carly jumped out of her seat and hugged her. "Oh, I'm so excited and thrilled! I can't wait to begin our new life."

"So, when are we leaving?" Carly's excitement rubbed off onto her.

"Next week. Now, be careful, and listen to me. Don't tell him about the baby nor the money. Got it? Just act normal, okay?"

"Yes."

"I want you to go home and pack a bag or two and bring them over to my place." Carly pulled her keys out of her purse, removed one key from the ring and handed it to Fausta. "Here. This is my apartment key. Brings your bags to my apartment today. Oh, and you do have a passport, right?"

"Oh yes, I had it done when I got married in the hopes of going somewhere for our honeymoon."

"Perfect." Carly stood. "I've got to get to work. I'll ring you when my flight is booked. I'll book one for you as well."

"Wait, do your colleagues know you're leaving?"

"Only one of my closest ones. Jessica knows but she's the only one." She hugged her friend. "Oh, I can't wait to leave. Cheerio!"

"Oh, I forgot to tell you…"

"What?" Fausta opened the café door.

"The city where I'll be working is called Melbourne. It's in Florida and it's close to NASA. Do you believe it?"

Fausta shook her head and laughed. "What are the odds?"

Chapter 2

500 miles away from New York

"How do you feel?"

Fausta stretched in the small coach seat. "Oh, I'm okay. What time is it?"

"It's about twelve our time." Carly yawned and pulled up her seat.

"Do you know where we are?" She lifted up the window shade but all she saw were white clouds below and the bluest sky she'd ever seen. It gave her a sense of hope and new beginnings.

"Well, last I heard…"

"Good morning ladies and gentlemen…" the speakers crackled with a pleasant man's voice. "We are about five hundred miles away from New York and we are scheduled to land in JFK around eight pm Eastern time." And there was silence.

"There you have it." Carly straightened up and pulled her table down. "Oh, by the way, we're going back in time."

"Back?"

"Yes, sixteen hours to be exact."

"Well, isn't that something."

"Good evening ladies and gentlemen." A perky female voice greeted. "We will be serving dinner in a few minutes so please lower your tray tables."

Most of the passengers began moving around, fidgeting and some got up to go to the restroom. Even Fausta got up and made a b-line to the restroom.

"I'll go when you get back."

After the second trip made by the flight attendants to collect trash, the P.A. squawked again.

"Ladies and gentlemen, this is Captain John Morris speaking. We are beginning our descent into JFK. We should be landing in about twenty minutes. The local time is twenty fifteen. The weather in New York is quite different from Sydney. In fact, here full winter is in force on the contrary of Sydney where we are in full summer season. We're not down under anymore, mates."

The passengers laughed.

"So, if you were smart enough to pack a coat, you better get it out now cause you're gonna need it. The local temperature is five degrees Celsius."

This time the passengers gasped.

About twenty-five minutes later, "Flight attendants, please prepare for landing." The *fasten your seatbelt* light came on along with the classic beep.

"All right, here we go. We begin a new chapter. Are you ready?"

"Honestly, no but with you by my side, I can't go wrong." Fausta held her friend's hand and squeezed it tight.

"You'll...I mean we will be fine. I have a good job lined up and you transferred your money in a local bank...what's the name of that bank again?"

Fausta pulled out her passport that had a piece of paper folded inside it. "Ummm...it's called the Space Coast Credit Union."

"Ah okay and how much American dollars is it?"

"I think around twenty thousand."

"Well, that's a good start indeed."

"My plan is to start working as soon as I can. I don't want to be a burden."

Carly patted her friend's hand. "I know honey, you will. Don't worry about it now."

Fausta patted her tummy. She felt her baby move for the first time when she boarded the plane. "I'm not. I'm going to have the baby first and then I'm going to study so I can get a teaching degree. I've always wanted to teach."

"You're going to make a terrific teacher."

The plane touched down with a screech and a few slight bumps.

"We're in America now."

Fausta rubbed her belly again. "We are."

"How do you feel?"

"Excited…scared…hopeful…"

"Faussy, that's perfectly normal. I feel the same way, but if we stick together and believe that God's got this, nothing can go wrong."

Fausta took a deep breath and said a quick prayer. *Yes, He's got this.*

~~~~~~

Melbourne, Australia

Yelling, Jack banged on Vincenzo's door. "Where is she?"

Vincenzo got up from watching the telly and looked out the front window. He headed for the door but didn't open it. "What do you want Jack?"

"Vince, I'm looking for Faussy! I need to talk to her. Open up!"

"She's not here, Jack, go home!" Vincenzo held his hand on his front door, hoping that Jack would leave. Gabriella was standing at the arc of the kitchen, holding a butcher knife.

"Open this fucking door! Now! I want my wife!"

Vincenzo whispered to his wife. "Call the police."

Gabriella nodded. She picked up the cordless and dialed the police. She headed to the kitchen door and locked it while she waited for the police to answer.

"Go home, Jack, she's not here! I told you already."

Jack's rage increased the intensity of his banging. "I'm not going anywhere until I see my wife!"

"I'm telling you, she's not here!"

Jack banged again. "You're lying, old man! You're protecting her, you fool!"

After what seemed an eternity, a police cruiser pulled up and two officers ran up to Jack. They grabbed him, used a night stick to hit him in the back of his knees and brought him down. Then one of the officers handcuffed him.

"Let me go! I didn't do anything!"

"That's not what we heard." One of the officers read an arresting rights notation card he retrieved from his pocket. "You have the right to telephone or speak to a friend or relative to inform that person where you are and to ask him or her to be present during questioning. You also have the right to telephone or speak to a lawyer of your choice to inform the lawyer where you are and to arrange or attempt to arrange for the lawyer to be present during questioning. If you want to telephone or speak to any of these people, questioning will be delayed for a reasonable time for that purpose. Is there anyone you wish to telephone or speak to?

The following caution is required with respect to the right to silence: Before I ask you any questions, I must tell you that you have the right to remain silent. This means you do not have to say anything, answer any question, or make any statement unless you wish to do so. However, if you do say something or make a statement, it may later be used as evidence. Do you understand?"

By the time the officer was done, Jack knew he was being hauled off to jail. "I'm coming back! As soon as I get out, I'm coming back." He yelled as he was forced inside the back of the cruiser.

"Constable Welby here, can you please open the door, Mr. Benito?"

Vincenzo opened the door. "Hello." He spoke with a slight Italian accent. He cocked his head and managed to see his son in law in the cruiser as the door was shut.

"Are you all right?"

"Yes, we are." Gabriella stood right behind Vincenzo. She didn't have an accent. "Just shaken up."

"May I come in and ask you a few questions?"

"Yes, of course. Please."

With notepad in hand, the officer stepped into the hallway. "Very well, please tell me what happened."

"Well, I was in front of the telly, watching the game and suddenly I hear Jack's voice and pounding on my front door. I got up and looked out that window." Vincenzo pointed to the front living room window. "And I saw him. He was very angry and kept pounding on my front door. I honestly thought he was going to break it open."

"Yes, me too. I was so scared." Gabriella said.

"I see. What was he asking for?"

"He wanted to see our daughter, Fausta and I kept telling him she wasn't here."

"Is she here?"

"No, she isn't. You can check for yourself." Vincenzo moved to let the officer search, but he didn't.

"No need, I believe you, but tell me, why did he come here to look for her?"

"I honestly don't know. Whenever she had arguments with her husband, we always send her home."

"It was not the right thing to do," said Gabriella.

"What kind of arguments were they?"

At that point, the second officer joined her colleague inside the home. "Good day, I'm Constable Damien."

Fausta's parents greeted the female officer.

"So, what kind of arguments were they?"

"Ah, you know, young couple spats." He waved his hands in the air. "The usual stuff, you know?"

Constable Damien also had her pen and notepad out. "Mr. Benito, did your son-in-law put his hands on your daughter?"

Vincenzo was taken aback by that question. He knew where this was heading, but now that he had experienced Jack's violent side, maybe his daughter was right. He nodded.

"Is that a 'yes'?"

"Yes, she came over many times with bumps and bruises, but HE always sent her home!" she yelled. "I told you Vince! I told you he was beating her but NO, you didn't believe our daughter, NO, you believed that son of a bitch! Maledetto!"

"Now, Mrs. Benito, please tell us your side of the story?" Constable Damien wrote in her notebook.

"As soon as she got married, that bastard started to hit her. I wanted her to stay but he..." Gabriella pointed a finger in Vince's face, "kept saying no...it was not our problem...it was their problem...we shouldn't get involved...I begged him...but he wouldn't listen! Now, you see Vince, you see now? I was right! He's a brutal maniac and now who knows where Fausta is!"

"Oh, mio Dio! What have I done?" Vincenzo buried his face in his hands. "She could be in real danger."

"Mr. Benito, do you have any idea where your daughter might be?" Welby asked.

"I-I don't know…" he frowned. *Could this man have killed my daughter?*

"Mrs. Benito, how about you?" Welby turned to Gabriella.

"She called me on Monday to tell me she was going out of town for a few days."

"Did she tell you where she was going?" Constable Damien asked.

"No, she just said out of town."

"Huh, out of town could be anywhere, really."

"Mr. Benito, please give us your daughter's address so we can investigate."

"Yes, yes, of course but please let us know if you find anything."

"Of course, but I have one more question for you both, but it is quite harsh."

"Yes, what is it?"

"Do you have any reason to believe that your son in law may have killed your daughter?"

They both glared at Constable Welby, and both nodded.

At that point, the officers closed their notepads and left the Benito home.

The Benitos wept for their daughter like they had never wept before.

~~~~~~

With the testimony of the Benitos, along with work colleagues of Jack, he was convicted of domestic violence and received a three-month sentence. While serving his sentence, he got into several fights with fellow inmates which prolonged his sentence to one year. One of the fellow inmates he got into a fight with was the notorious Willie Byrd, a gang boss with a rap sheet as long as the Murry River. One night, Jack was paid a visit by Willie's minions.

"You pissed off the wrong bloke, mate." One of his assailants whispered in his ear while he was yanked out of his bunk, raped, and beaten to a pulp.

After that, Jack's visitors came more frequent even though he attempted to hold his temper, but underneath, as time went by, he fermented like a bottle of Moscato. When he was released two years later, the first thing he did was quietly search for Fausta.

Chapter 3

Melbourne, Florida

During a typical raging, Florida summer storm, on July 4th, 1998, Nora Gabriella Benito came into the world. From the very start, she was very quiet and mellow.

Fausta had worked at her 7-Eleven job just until the day before her birth. Her pregnancy had allowed her to work throughout the nine months since she hardly had any morning sickness or any other pregnancy symptoms. She worked by day and studied by night. By the time Nora was born, Fausta had graduated Brevard Teacher College with her Bachelor's. She decided to stay at her 7-Eleven job until she received a decent job offer, preferably from one of the major schools that were found on the Space Coast.

Fausta was able to put a down payment on a small house in Ixora Park with the money she brought from Australia. Carly was co-owner since she was the one who had a good-paying full-time job. The situation was working out well thanks to a bank clerk that Fausta met when she opened her bank account at the Space Coast Credit Union. "Invest this money in a home. You won't regret it." She did as she was advised, and now she was partial co-owner with the only friend she had ever had, Carly McIntyre.

"Oh my God, Faussy, she's the most beautiful baby I've ever seen." Carly patted the newborn's head. "Congratulations! I'm so happy for you." She spoke quietly so she wouldn't wake up Nora.

"You didn't have to do that." Fausta pointed at the huge pink teddy bear that Carly brought into the room along with balloons, candies and a huge greeting card.

"Yes, I did. You deserve all of this and more. You've accomplished so much in such little time." She gently hugged her best friend. "I'm so proud of you."

Fausta glowed with pride and joy even though she was stinky and sweaty from the labor. She never thought she would have made it but here she was, holding this sweet bundle of hope, her best friend in the world by her side, and her abusive husband far, far away.

"I'm so happy I could explode." Tears streamed down her cheeks fogging the view of her daughter's face.

Carly sat next to Fausta on the bed and looked attentively at the baby. "I hate to say this but she's the spitting…"

"Image of Jack, yes, I noticed it immediately."

Both women stayed in silence for a few moments, while taking in the beauty and innocence of the newborn.

"Do you ever think of him?"

Fausta raised her eyes to Carly. "I do...you know...sometimes I think...if only Jack had been a different kind of husband...maybe we could be celebrating the birth of our daughter at home, in Australia..." she looked down at her daughter. "Oh, I don't know...I'm just being sentimental I guess."

"I don't think so. It's natural for a woman to want to share this joy with the man of her life and he's the only many you've ever known." She stroked her friend's sweaty hair away from her face. "Just know that I'm here for you, kay? I'm not goin' anywhere. You got that?"

"Where is she?" The question was posed by a young man who walked into the hospital room along with several of Fausta's work colleagues. They slowly and silently walked into the hospital room, carrying flowers, candy, balloons, and toys for the newborn.

After everyone made their way in, all the gifts were set up anywhere there was room, and soon the room was brightened up by colorful greeting cards, flowers, balloons, and various stuffed animals.

Fausta was able to stay home for three full months until she received an offer from Space Shuttle Elementary. She found an elderly lady who lived a few homes down the street who offered to take care of Nora while Fausta was at school. Fausta was very pleased at how things were coming together but in the back of her mind a bit of trepidation was stored from her life in Australia. A few months later, while she was changing Nora and preparing her for bed, she gently promised:

"I'm always going to take care of you, my love. I'm never going to let anything bad happen to you. This I promise you." She sung her a lullaby as the young girl slowly sailed into Lala land.

~~~~~~

Melbourne, Australia

Jack was finally released from the penitentiary in July of 2002. Almost immediately, he headed for the Benito's home. He rang the doorbell and a little blond haired-blue eyed child holding a white stuffed bunny opened the door. He wondered who the child was. Was it Fausta's?

"Well, hello lad. Is your mama home?"

The child turned. "Mummy!" He screamed at the top of his lungs.

He heard footsteps, and a young woman who had the exact same features as her son appeared cleaning her hands with a dish towel. A look of fear painted her face as she quickly moved the child behind her. "Who are you?"

As he did when he was a teenager, Jack raised his eyebrows and showed his pearly whites. "G-mornin' ma'am, my name is Jack. I'm looking for Mr. Benito."

She shoved her son into the hallway, closed the door as she stepped onto the veranda. "Oh, they moved away about three years ago now."

"Oh, I see." He figured he'd scared them and that they'd be gone by the time he was released. "Do you know where they went?"

"I think in Kilsyth, but I'm not completely sure."

Jack didn't want to bother her any more than he needed to. "Thanks much. I'll be running off now."

He didn't so much than turn around and the woman closed the door and locked it firmly while a shiver went down her spine.

"Kilsyth eh? I'll 'ave to remember that." He wasn't surprised to find out that the Benitos moved away. "Ha, ha, I must've scared the bigibees outta 'em." He smiled coyly.

As he drove back to Melbourne, he tried to remember Fausta's friend's name. "Was it Carol?" He shook his head. "Nah. Maybe Cathy?" He shook his head again. "Come on bloke, think!" He slammed the palm of his hand against his forehead. "Was it Karen? No, no, no!" He hit himself a few more times. "Carla maybe?" He stopped at a red light and saw a red head cross the road walking a huge German

Shephard. "Carly! That's it! Carly!" As the light turned green, he blasted the volume just as his favorite group *Men at Work* were singing their most famous song, *Who Can It Be Now?* "I know who it is now!"

~~~~~~

"Any mail from Fausta?" Gabriella asked.

"Not today." Vince replied with a frown. "But she'll write soon. I can feel it."

Over the last five years, Fausta had written them five times, and all were postcards. The first came from Washington DC with a brief note that said "I'm in America now. Please don't look for me." The second came from New York with another brief note that said, "I'm pregnant and will be having your grandchild soon." The third was a photo-postcard with a picture of Nora on the front and a sentence that said, "Meet your granddaughter, Nora." The fourth was another photo-postcard with a picture of Nora on her first birthday, with cake all over her hands. And the last and fifth photo postcard was taken on her first day of kindergarten and another brief note on the back that said, "First day of kindergarten."

"I hope you're right. I think Nora may be starting elementary soon. She should be turning six soon." Gabriella was walking Spike, a French Bulldog who was around the age of Nora. They got him from a breeder who lived in the countryside of Gowanbrae, where their retirement village was. They told the new owner of their house that they were moving to Kilsyth because Jack would be looking for them when he got out. He'd promised them as he was being hauled away.

Vince put his arm around his wife's shoulder. "Yes, I'm sure of it."

"You know, I'm so glad she left."

"Oh? I thought you were angry?"

"I was yes, but now that I know she's safe in America, I'm glad that she was able to save herself and our precious Nora."

"I can't help but blame myself for that. If only I had realized that he was abusing her, I would have demanded they divorce. Damn!"

"Oh, don't beat yourself up, Vince, you didn't know, and I suspected something but never thought he was that abusive." Spike pulled a bit harder than usual. "Spike no!" and the pooch did as he was commanded.

"Well, life goes on I suppose. Come now…let's go have lunch."

~~~~~~

Melbourne, Florida

About a year after 9-11, a police officer came in to make a presentation. The entire school, including teachers, were assembled in the gym. He was going to discuss what to do in case of a terrorist attack. There had been a lot of pressure from the Federal Government to local governments to train the citizenship of the perils of terrorist attacks. As the officer whizzed through his presentation, covering all the possible scenarios, Fausta was imagining her own terrorist attack but not by some angry Islamist, rather—her ex-husband. She ran away with his money, and she started thinking how angry he could have become. *Would he look for me? Would he threaten my parents?* A shiver went down her spine. She decided when she got home, she would call her parents. As the day progressed, she became more and more anxious and couldn't wait to get home.

When she finally arrived home, she put Nora down for a nap, but the girl wasn't having any of it.

"Oh, Nora, today was the day you are going to misbehave." Fausta put Nora on the carpet and set up all her favorite toys. As soon as Nora found an interest in the animal farm toys, Fausta quickly went to her room to get the phone. She dialed the number without looking it up. She could never forget her parents' number. The international ring was noticeably different than a local ring.

After a few rings, the voice mail box kicked in. "You have reached the Benito family. Please leave a message and we will get back with you as soon as we can. Thank you."

"Mamma." She said as she hung up. She looked at her clock. It was 4:03 pm so it would have been 8:03 am over there. "I'll wait." She said as she headed to check on Nora.

Around 5:25 she dialed them again and once again, it went to voicemail.

"Shit!" She quietly cursed so her daughter wouldn't hear it. She headed to the kitchen to start dinner. *I'll call them later on. Maybe they went out to run some errands. They'll be back for lunch. I hope.*

Carly went to bed early that evening. She had a deadline at work and wanted to get a head start for the morning. As soon as she was in her room, Fausta dialed her parents.

"Hello?" Vince responded.

"Papà?"

"Fausta? Figlia mia, sei proprio tu?"

"Si, sono io. Come stai?" Somehow her Italian came rushing back.

"Fausta? Fausta, is that you?" Gabriella asked speaking into the phone she took from her husband.

"Yes mamma, it's me."

"Oh, my Lord! Our prayers have been answered! Where are you?"

"I'm so sorry Mamma, but I can't tell you." She really wanted to, though.

"Oh, I understand. Better safe than sorry."

Vince took the phone. "Fausta, I'm so sorry. I didn't realize he was hitting you. I'm so sorry figlia mia!" He broke down.

"Papà, it's okay, really, I'm safe now and so is Nora."

"Oh, Nora, what a sweet girl. Thank you for sending the photos. She's beautiful. She looks just like you."

"Yes, she does now but when she was a baby, she looked like him."

"Where are you, Fausta? Can you say?"

"No, Papà, I'd rather not if that's okay?"

"Sure, sure."

She heard the disappointment in his voice. "I can tell you this, I'm a teacher."

"A teacher?"

"Oh, she always wanted to be a teacher." Gabriella cried into the phone over Vince's shoulder.

"Yes. I have a good life. I'm happy. Really."

"That's all we want to know. You're safe in America! And that's a dream come true for millions of people. You know, I don't care where you are, as long as you are in America and you're happy. Basta!"

"Grazie Papà." Fausta wiped her eyes with her cardigan sleeve. "I must ask; where is Jack?"

"Last I saw, he was being hauled off to jail."

"Jail?"

"Si, figlia mia, si."

Gabriella took the phone from Vince's hand. "I'll continue from here. So, a couple of days after you left, Jack came over, pounding on the door, demanding you come out."

"Oh, that must have been frightening."

"You don't know the half of it. He pounded harder and harder and finally the police came and arrested him."

"Good."

"Oh yes. He was away for over three years."

"Three years? Why so long?"

"We don't know why. Every time I called the courthouse just to know when he would be out, they told me six more months, then six more months again, and in the end, he stayed for over three years."

"That's incredible. He must have done something else to make things worse."

"Knowing now that he was a violent man, I assume so."

"So, did he come back after he got out?"

"We don't know because we sold the house and moved to a senior village. Gowanbrae village to be exact."

"Bravi! Smart move!"

"I know, and we told the buyers that we were moving to a different village, which is very far away from Melbourne."

Fausta really wanted to tell her parents that she lived in Melbourne too, but she bit her tongue. "Okay, I must go. It's getting late, and I have school tomorrow. I wanted to make sure you were all right and I can sleep easy now."

"Fausta, will you call again?"

"I can't promise that, but I can promise to send you photos of Nora, okay."

"Grazie, figlia mia, grazie! We love you so much!"

Vince grabbed the phone. "Yes, and please give a big kiss to Nora for us, okay?"

"Yes Papà, I will. Good night." And she hung up.

Vince and Gabriella hugged each other.

"She called! She called! Oh, I can't wait to tell my friends."

"No, Gabriella, no! We mustn't. Eh, you never know. We must protect our little girl and our beautiful granddaughter."

Gabriella's excitement deflated like a flat tire. "You're right, you're right."

"I know. I will not allow that figlio di puttana to hurt my family. I will die first."

Chapter 4

Melbourne, Australia

Jack searched high and low for Carly, but the more he searched, the more she was unfindable. He knew they were neighbors, but when he went to Carly's parents' house, they too, were gone. They had moved into a retirement village, but the new owners didn't know where they went. It was suspicious to him that both the Benitos and the McIntyres had moved away to retirement villages. He couldn't help but wonder if they did it on purpose.

He started a new search of all the school mates Fausta had but that didn't take him anywhere. It made his blood boil.

One day, after work, he noticed a lot across the street from the condominiums he was working. It was fenced off and there was a huge "Coming Soon" sign. Curious, he walked across so he could read the fine print. "Myer Department Store to open in Spring of 2008." Next to the announcement was a design of how the store was going to look like. Something went off in his head. "That's right, Myer. That's where Carly worked right out of school."

He got in his old heap and drove to the Myer store that was in his old neighborhood. He parked it and went inside. He looked at every woman who would have been remotely familiar, but he didn't recognize anyone. He got on the escalator and took a look around there, nothing. He got on the escalator again and went up to the third and last floor. He walked around and saw a familiar face. His grin expanded from cheek to cheek.

"Jessica? Jessica Richards? Is that you?"

She didn't recognize him at first but when she did, her face turned dark. "Jack, right?"

"Yes, you remembered." He started flirting with her.

"I can't talk, I've got work to do." She wanted to get away from him as fast as she could. He had a reputation, and she wanted no part of him.

"Wait, please, I'd like only five minutes, please." He didn't touch her but simply kept her from leaving.

Jessica saw that there were plenty of people around so she figured he wouldn't do anything rash. "Sure, okay."

"I'm looking for Carly. Carly McIntyre. Do you remember her?"

"Yes, I do why?"

"Well, she was Fausta's best friend, and I think she may know where my wife is."

Jessica was the only person Carly confided in before she left for the US and she made her a promise. She hesitated. "Sorry, I don't know where she is. I can't help you." She swiftly walked away to a customer who was searching for a clerk to help him.

Jack grinned. *That's okay darlin', I'll see you later.*

Jack had made Jessica uneasy. So, she asked one of her male colleagues to accompany her to her car. "Thanks Thomas, I appreciate this." She unlocked her car and got into the driver's seat.

"Don't mention it." Thomas watched as she drove away.

She pushed in her favorite CD and raised the volume.

"Aww, did I make you uncomfortable, lassie?" Jack whispered in her ear as he put his knife to her throat.

"Uh…what? What are you…" Jessica looked into the rear view mirror.

"Shut up you bitch! Keep drivin' until I order ya ta stop!" He pushed the knife under her chin.

"O…Okay…" Her pulse raced as she gripped the steering wheel until her fingers were white. She felt his knife almost tearing into her jugular.

Jack's knife was firm. "Now, pull over there!" he commanded. He got out first. "Get out!"

With trembling hands, she unbuckled her seat belt and raising her hands to the night sky, she got out.

He grabbed her by her bleached-blonde hair and pulled her to where nobody can see. He slammed her against a large pine tree trunk and once again, placed the knife on her neck.

"Now, tell me where she is?"

"W-will you let me go if I do?"

Jack smiled devilishly and eased up on the pressure. "I promise."

"They-they went to America." She rubbed her neck.

"They?" he was confused.

"Yes, Carly and Fausta went to America, together."

Jack stepped back. "Is that so?"

"Yes." Jessica started walking towards her car while making sure he didn't make any moves. "Can-can I go now?" she took one step forward and waited for Jack's reaction.

Jack waved her to walk by. "Of course." But as soon as she had her back to him, he dug his knife into her spine and then turned the blade on a 90-degree angle. He held on to her as she collapsed to the ground. He removed the knife, and as he slid it into his jacket pocket, he cut his finger fairly deep. "Shit." He pulled out his handkerchief and wrapped it around the cut as quickly as he could. Several drops of blood landed on Jessica's brown slacks.

He wrapped his hand as best as he could and began walking down the road. He took her there purposely so he could walk home after the deed was done.

While he walked, he used his cell phone to dial an old buddy of his, Tony O'Malley, who was an expert with computers and the internet.

"Y'ello."

"Tony, Jack 'ere."

Tony wasn't happy to hear from him. Jack was bad news, any day of the year. "Yeah, what?"

"I need a favor mate."

A "Cha-ching" sound went off in his head. "I'm listening."

"I need your expertise to find a woman."

"Go on."

"She a friend of my wife and she may know where my wife is. Her name is Carly McIntyre, and it seems she and my wife ran away together to the US."

"The US eh? That's a big country mate, it's gonna be a quid."

"Name your price."

Tony had him where he wanted him. He knew this bloke wouldn't hesitate to pay whatever price to find his wife. "A thousand." He didn't ask. It was a demand.

Jack hesitated. "Fine. Say where and when?"

"I'm gonna need a few days. I'll put everything on a flash drive for ya."

"What's that?"

"It's a little storage device about the size of two blunts."

"And what am I supposed to do with it?"

"I'll show ya when I see ya. Gladstone Park, Friday night around ten. One minute after and I'm gone."

"Yeah. I'll be there." Jack's thoughts were already working on eliminating Tony.

"Oh, and Jack, don't even think about takin' me out cause I back up everything I do. Got it?"

Well, there goes that thought. "Yeah, yeah, got it."

~~~~~~

Inspector Damien roamed around the crime scene. She had forensics collect everything they could possibly find but there wasn't much left since the body was exposed to rain most of the night.

"Who called it in?"

"A jogger. Female. Around 7:15."

"Did you get her name?"

"Yes, and she's willing to make a statement."

"Good man." Inspector Damien patted the young constable on the back.

"All right everyone, gather 'round." She waited for the entire crew to create a circle around her. "I want photographs, and lots of them. I want the car torn apart and every inch searched. I want a detailed autopsy. How soon can I get it?"

"About a week, Inspector."

She knew well that it was going to be longer than that but hopefully, since this was a murder, she may get lucky. "A bit too much, but I want it to be thorough, so I'll take it. Please put it on my desk as soon as you have it."

"Yes, Inspector."

April Damien wasn't the only one who'd been promoted. Her old partner Kevin Welby had also made his way up the ranks.

"Oh, speak of the devil."

Kevin got out of his unmarked car and headed towards his colleague.

"Hey April, how are you? Long time, eh?" He gave her a hug. He always had a crush on her but for some reason, she was never interested.

"Ah, dear Kevin, thanks for coming."

"Always happy to help." He looked around. "So, what's going on?"

"A woman was stabbed last night," she said as the black body bag was hoisted into the van.

"Do you know who she is?"

"Yes, Jessica Jones. That vehicle belongs to her. All her information is on her ownership card."

Kevin looked around and wrote on his notebook. "Looks like the rain made things more difficult."

"Unfortunately." She sighed.

"Now, April, don't be discouraged. We've done it before, and we can do it again."

"I suppose." She wasn't convinced.

"Come on, let me buy you lunch." He put his notebook away and headed for his car. "Come on!"

"All right. I've gotta wait anyway."

~~~~~~

Jack slid the flash drive into the USB port and waited for the window to pop up, just like Tony explained. He clicked on the "Open Files" button and there was one file there. He double clicked it to open it and the document took over the screen.

"Blimey!"

The document was filled with information. It had the date when they left, what flight they took, and where they landed.

"Orlando, Florida."

Then Jack read on to see where they settled, what Carly did for a living, and what Fausta did for a living.

50

"Well, look at that, there's a Melbourne in Florida. What are the odds?"

He printed out the entire document, folded it so it would fit in his pocket, removed the flash drive, and left the library.

While he was on his bus route, he pulled out the document to view it again. "Florida. I'm gonna need at least five grand to get there." He whispered quietly to himself. He didn't want to grab the attention of anybody. He had to figure something out and fast.

~~~~~~

Two months later, there was a break in the case but there was something bothering her, and she couldn't put her finger on it. April picked up all the folders, placed them in her backpack and went to Kevin's station.

A young Constable asked when she walked in, "Inspector Damien, can I help you?"

"Yes. Is Inspector Welby in? I need to see him." She drummed her fingers impatiently on his desk.

"Yes. He's in his office."

"Thanks." She quickly headed to Kevin's office.

When she arrived, Kevin was on the phone, so she sat in the first chair and waited until he was done, tapping her right foot. She tended to do that when she was nervous.

"Okay, see you around five. Bye." He hung up and gave April a reassuring smile. "I'm all yours." He meant that if she wanted it.

She opened her bag and pulled out files. "Okay, so you remember Jessica Richard's case?" She handed him a sheet of paper.

"Yes. We've been stuck on motive for two months now."

"Right. Well, turns out she's Carly McIntyre's old work colleague."

Kevin snatched the paper. "And I suppose you're going to tell me who this Carly McIntyre is."

"Yes. I did some digging and Carly worked with Jessica at Myer back in the day."

"The department store?"

"Yes, exactly."

Kevin handed the paper back to April. "And?"

"I also found out that Carly is Fausta Rinaldi's best friend since childhood." She pulled out a couple of photos from the two girls secondary school days.

Kevin glared at the photos and thought about that name for a few "Rinaldi? Doesn't ring a bell."

April sat back and cracked a sly smile. "Of course not, because Rinaldi is her married name. Her maiden name is Benito." She let that sink in.

"Benito? Ummmm…"

"Here, this may juggle your memory." She pulled the report they had made together back in 2002.

Kevin read the report thoroughly and it looked like a light went off in his head. "Yes, the violent son in law who and was looking for his wife…"

"…whose name was Fausta…Fausta Rinaldi."

"So, are you suggesting that son in law…what was his name again…"

"Jack Rinaldi. And yes, I'm suggesting exactly that. He got resourceful and found Jessica who was Carly's workplace colleague and Carly was his wife's best friend."

"Yes! Brilliant! We've got to find this bloke and now!" He got up and grabbed his phone and weapon. "Come on, I'm buying lunch."

April followed him out. Finally. A break in the case.

"Leslie, I want everything you can find me on this man." He handed his assistant a photo of Jack when he'd first been arrested. "His name is Giacomo Rinaldi, but he goes by Jack. And search these two as well, please." He handed her a photo of Carly and Fausta.

"Yes, sir."

"I'm going out, but I'll be back in a couple of hours. I want everything on my desk by then. Got it?"

"Yep."

Once they were in the parking lot, April asked: "Do you think it's a good idea to have her research, Jack?"

Kevin was a bit surprised. "She's my best researcher. I promise you, she can find the needle in the haystack. You just watch."

"All right, if you say so." She climbed into her SUV.

"Do I detect an inkling of jealousy?" He climbed into the passenger side.

"What? No, no, not at all." She dismissed him but she was disappointed that he asked some woman to look up a past arrestee of theirs. She desired to work with him on this.

Kevin wasn't convinced but didn't react. He was hoping that this was the break he was waiting for but in their relationship, not in the case.

Exactly two hours later, both Kevin and April were sifting through the paperwork that Leslie had neatly placed on his desk.

"Says here both women left Australia in late 1997."

"Does it say where they went?" Kevin looked at April through his readers.

She looked at him thinking how he had tastefully aged. "America."

"Well, that's a big country. Can you be more specific?"

"Says here Carly was offered an Engineering position at RGF Space Solutions."

"Where is their headquarters?"

"Well, therein lies the problem. This firm has affiliates throughout the United States."

"Really? How many affiliates?"

"Let's see…Sacramento, California, Austin, Texas, Birmingham, Alabama, Nashville, Tennessee, Louisville, Kentucky and Melbourne, Florida."

"Melbourne? There's a Melbourne in Florida?"

"Seems like it."

Kevin scratched his chin. "I'll bet you anything, they live there."

"I would agree."

"What exactly does this company do?"

"From what I can tell, they are a contractor for NASA."

"NASA eh? Isn't that interesting." Kevin leaned back in his chair.

"Oh, here's their employee roster."

Kevin leaned forward, "Is her name on there?"

"Negative."

Kevin looked at his watch. "What time is it over there?"

"Well, let's go check the clocks out there."

"Capital idea."

They both got up and headed for the clocks in the main office.

"All right, well it's about 2:30 here so it's 10:30 in New York. Let's call them."

"No, that's 22:30."

"Ah, okay then, we'll call them early tomorrow then."

"Okay, I'll be here around 7:00."

"All right, now let's look at Jack's history."

April sifted through some other papers. "Says here his latest address is…get this…walking distance from Jessica's murder site."

"Really, well let's go pay him a visit, shall we?"

~~~~~~

"Thanks man." Jack handed the shady, young, pierced, man full of tattoos a wad of cash.

He looked at Jack with his beady eyes and counted the cash. He counted it very quickly and placed it inside a cash box, locking it with a key hanging from a chain around his neck. He gave Jack a manilla envelope and raised his chin a couple of times gesturing him to leave.

Jack didn't have to be told twice. He knew the goods were of the best counterfeit quality there was. As he walked down the street, he pulled out his brand spanking new fake passport along with a fake birth certificate and a fake temporary work VISA for the US. All had his new name, Jack Reynolds. He nodded in satisfaction and appeasement. "I'm gonna try this puppy out right now." He walked into a travel agency.

"Morning sir. How can I help?" the pretty bleached blonde asked.

He once again turned on his charm. "I need to go to the US…for business…can you help?" His pearly whites were his finishing touch to his business.

"Yes, of course, sir, let me look for you." She began tapping on her keyboard. "When were you looking to leave?"

"As soon as possible. I've got some important business to attend to."

"Very good sir, and where exactly in the US were you looking to go?"

"Florida."

"Oh, how lovely. Florida is quite pretty this time of year." She kept babbling on about Florida's theme parks, beaches and the Kennedy Space Center.

About three minutes had passed, but for Jack, it seemed much more. He began tapping his index finger on the counter.

"The earliest flight to Orlando, Florida is in a couple of days. Would that be all right sir?"

He wanted something earlier, but this would have had to do for now. "Yes, of course. How much?"

"Let me see…round trip from Melbourne, Australia to Orlando Florida, stopping in Los Angeles and New York would be $1785.00, sir."

Jack turned his back to her, pulled out some cash, counted it, and placed it on the counter. "Book it." Even though he was planning on not returning to Australia, he paid for a round trip.

~~~~~~

"Nothing here." Kevin looked around.

"This place is empty. No clothes, no nothing."

"He must know we're on to him."

"Probably." She looked around some more in the hopes of finding something. She saw a crumpled piece of paper behind the waste basket. "What's this?" She flattened it as best as she could and found an address in a shady part of town. "Look, it's an address of a tattoo shop on Little Queen Street."

"Brilliant! Let's go!"

They both shot out the tiny apartment, got into Kevin's undercover SUV, snapped on sirens and lights and off they went. While Kevin drove, April called into her station asking for information on the Tattoo shop. Seconds later, she was informed that it wasn't only a tattoo shop, but it also provided fake documents for anyone willing to pay. "That bastard is getting a fake passport."

"Yes, he's probably going to the US."

"To kill his wife!"

"Well, shit!"

Now it seemed like they couldn't get there fast enough.

"You! Get out here now!"

The same dude who served Jack came out of the dark back room. "What you want?"

"Did you see this man?" Kevin shoved a photo of Jack into the tattooed guy's face.

He glanced at it and quickly said "No."

Kevin moved the photo closer and asked again.

"I said no! Now get this thing outta my face!" He pushed Kevin's hand away.

"We know what shady business you're in here, so you better talk!" April demanded.

"Sure, I'd be happy to help right after you show me your warrant." He folded his arms to await a document that didn't exist.

"Come on man, help us out. This is a really bad dude. He killed a young woman in cold blood." April showed him another photo of Jessica. "Look at her. Don't you think she deserves justice?"

She was nice looking. He thought but his expression said otherwise. "Of course, I do, but after you show me a warrant. Sorry mates." Then he gestured toward the door. "Now, if you don't mind, I'm a busy man."

Slamming his fists on the counter, Kevin picked up the two photos and shoved them into his pocket.

"Bloody waste of time!"

Defeated, they exited the shop.

"Now what?"

"We get a proper search warrant." April headed for the SUV.

"Wait." Kevin stopped her. "Look over there."

"What, the travel agency?"

"Yes."

"Do you think he would have been so stupid as to book a flight from that one?"

"I've known worse dickbrains than this one." He smirked. "Come on, let's give it a try." He crossed the street and headed for the travel agency.

She shrugged her shoulders and followed him.

"Good day." The blonde greeted them cheerfully.

They both presented their badges. "I'm Inspector Damien, and this is Inspector Welby."

"Yes, inspectors, how may I help you?" Her tone wasn't so cheerful anymore. It was no secret that this part of town didn't take a liking to cops.

Kevin pulled out a photo of Jack. "By chance, did this man come here within the past week or so."

I knew it! She thought. She just got confirmation that he was suspicious when he paid cash for his ticket. She didn't want to say anything. But she didn't want to get in trouble with the law either. "Um, yes, he was here."

"When?"

"Last Thursday, I believe."

April's eyes lit up. "What did he want?"

"A ticket to the US."

"Where in the US exactly?"

"Florida, I believe."

"When is he leaving?" Kevin asked.

"He left last Saturday."

Both inspectors frowned.

"Bloody hell!"

"Thanks." April sadly said as they left the agency. "Now what?"

"The only thing we can do is send the State of Florida an international BOLO through INTERPOL."

"Will it help our case?"

"Probably not." He got into his SUV and slammed the door.

April shook her head. "Ripper! We all know how that's going to end, don't we?"

"Yeah. Come on, I'll buy you a round."

Chapter 5

Melbourne, Florida

"So, can I have a party, Mommy?"

Fausta took a deep breath. She really didn't want to deal with her daughter's request, but it was her birthday.

"Come on Fausta, it'll be fine."

"Please Mommy?" She showed her mother the most dreadful puppy dog eyes. "Please?"

"Fine." Fausta gave up. Between the both of them, she didn't have a choice. She shook her head and shrugged her shoulders. "But…"

Nora jumped up and down and clapped her hands as she ran "eights" around both women. "But what?"

"Don't forget what I've taught you. Always be on guard and be ready to escape like we talked."

"I promise, Mommy, I promise." She hugged her mother. "I'm going to call all my friends." She raced into the family room to begin her calling spree.

Carly leaned in Fausta's direction and bumped shoulders with her. "She'll be fine. Stop worrying."

Fausta had tears rolling down. "She's grown up so fast. How did this happen?"

"It's called life, sweety."

"All right, well, I guess I'll give Chucky Cheese a call."

"Oh, I've got a better idea."

"What?"

"Andretti Thrill Park."

"What's that?"

"Get this. They can drive go-carts. Do you believe it?"

"Go carts? Isn't that a bit dangerous?"

"No way. They've got it down to a science. They also have party rooms, video games and mini golf. It's safe with armed security guards and it's fenced in."

"Okay, fine. But note, this is the second cave for today. Don't ever say I say 'no' too much ever again. Got it?"

"Yeah, yeah."

"So, are you bringing that dashing young cop of yours?"

"Oh yes, Terrance will be there for sure and he's bringing a friend...maybe you'll open up to a new relationship?"

"No, Carly, you know the rules. Don't set me up. I only want what's best for Nora, I don't have time for a fling."

"Come on Faussy, you never have fun. It's all Nora here and Nora there. What about Fausta?"

"No, and that's final." She folded her arms to assure the no sunk into her best friend's head.

Carly frowned. "Well, there you go again saying no."

"Two out of three ain't bad. Be happy."

The two women giggled. They had a great life for themselves, and they worked very hard to get there. Carly had made it to a managerial position and Fausta had a high school teaching position for Melbourne High School, and she adored teaching teenagers. She enjoyed their spunk, their fearlessness and their open minds. The only damper on their life was the fear of Jack finding out where they were and finding out about Nora. There was no way that Fausta would let that man touch her. She was fiercely protective and rightly so. Both mother and daughter had learned how to shoot and Fausta applied for her concealed carry permit almost a year ago and bought a Glock 26 9mm as soon as she received her permit.

~~~~~~

Jack settled in easily enough. He found a small apartment off of US1 and University Blvd and a job at F.I.T., through a private cleaning company, as a custodian. He was quite popular with the students because of his Aussie accent and turns out he was very popular with the female students because of his physique and charm. He was very careful to stay under the radar. He didn't want anyone looking into his past. He worked, went to the school gym to keep himself fit and trim and he went home. Even though he received many succulent offers from the female students and professors, he promptly and politely refused. His only plan was to find Fausta and convince her to return to Australia with him. He believed in his heart that she still loved him especially if he convinced her, he was a changed man. But damn it, he'd been here almost a year now and finding his wife was like finding a needle in a haystack. He couldn't imagine she looked exactly as she did when she left him. Maybe she changed her hair color. Maybe she gained weight. Maybe she was married. Oh, in that case, he would kill both of them. No other man was going to have her, only him.

"Hey Jack, do you want to join us for drinks later on?"

"Yeah, sure mate. I'm always up for a round eh?"

"Cool. We'll see you at Hooters around nine, okay?"

"Yeah, I'll see ya there."

~~~~~~

A beautiful blonde approached their table showcasing her full bosom.

"All right boys, what'll it be?"

"Huh, I'll have you later on girly." Jack commented while reaching up to her breasts but then he froze throwing both hands in the air like it was a "stick up". The others laughed and ignored him and without skipping a beat they ordered their drinks. Jack slowly got up and headed for the back of the dining room where a small group of women were cackling away. One in particular caught his eye. The women didn't notice him but when he touched one of them on the shoulder, "Fausta, is that you?"

She jumped out of her seat. "Who are you? What do you want from me?" she stepped away from him keeping a safe distance. She didn't like the looks of him.

It's not her. He was disappointed and became angry, but he kept his cool. He bowed slightly, apologized and went back to his table.

Did my eyes deceive me? He sat back down. Ah, it's too bloody dark in here. "Sorry, gents, gotta run." He got up and took off. He was too angry to stay and get drunk. He had to let off some steam, so he headed for the school gym and worked out until he was too tired to think.

"So, what happened the other night man?" Sanjiv asked. He was an Engineering student from India with not very many friends in Florida. On top of looking like a typical East Indian geek, he was thin, wore thick black glasses and was very shy in his demeanor.

"Oh, it was nothin'. I wasn't feeling so good." He lied which always came easy for him.

"So, listen, there's this go-cart placed called Andretti Thrill Park just south of here. Are you interested? I heard it's lots of fun."

Sanjiv's invite sparked his interest. "Go-cart, eh? Yeah, sounds interesting mate."

"Nice. How about this Friday?"

"Aren't you celebrating the fourth man?"

"Nah, I'm from India. I don't really care about the fourth. I'm just here for a few years to finish my studies."

"Yeah, I hear ya. Sure. Okay, how about I meet you at the Seven-Eleven around eight?"

"Nice, see you then man." He began to walk away. "We can walk from there. It's a very short walk, you'll see."

~~~~~~

On the evening of the fourth around nine-twenty, Sanjiv went inside the building and Jack followed behind.

"What the 'ell!" he exclaimed as a five-year-old ran right into him.

"Sorry." He said and disappeared into the crowd of little kids that seemed sparse everywhere.

"Hey Sanjiv, why are there so many rug rats here?" Jack wasn't fond of children.

"Oh, probably some birthday or something." He waved them off. "Don't worry about them. Just follow me."

"All right." He followed Sanjiv trying to avoid the little tykes as much as possible. They headed outside towards the racetrack and the go-carts roared by sounding their engines loudly. The kids in this section were older than the ones inside and they were all patiently lined up for their turn on the go-carts.

Sanjiv bought the tickets and headed to the end of the queue.

"That's a long line mate."

"I know right? This is the only downside to this place, the wait but I promise it will be worth every second."

"Right then. You stay in line, and I'll get us some beer."

"Oh no! You can't wait in line and drink. If they catch you, they won't let you on the carts."

"Seriously? Geez!" Jack's patience was quickly dwindling. There was no way he was waiting that long. Besides, it sounded like a summer storm was brewing on the horizon. "All right then, you wait here, and I'll go inside for a quick beer."

"Sure, I'll text you when it's our turn."

Jack waved and headed inside, making a B-Line for the bar and ordered a Corona. From where he sat, he had a good outlook on the queue and was able to run out as Sanjiv got closer. The local channel was running a special on the

Fourth of July festivities from the White House. He loved how Americans were so patriotic. That's one thing Aussies lacked. His eyes shifted from the TV to the queue outside. Then his attention suddenly shifted to two women in a go-cart. They were laughing out loud and seemed like they were having a great time. His eyes followed them as they drove on the speedway and lost them when they entered the colorful lit up short tunnel. As soon as they came out, he focused on them again. They looked awfully familiar. One was blondish and wearing a jean jacket while the other was a brunette wearing a tight tank top that showcased her perfect breasts. He got up, gulped his beer down and headed outside where he could get a closer look but staying back enough so the two women wouldn't notice him. "Could it be?" he whispered to himself. As they came roaring by the curve, he recognized them and almost fell over the curb.

"Blimey!" he shouted and got a few weird looks by a few teenagers. He sneered at them.

Carly and Fausta were having such a terrific time riding the go-cart, they were completely oblivious of the familiar man staring at them. When their ride ended, they were helped off the go-cart by a young man who guided them off the track. Fausta felt cold for some strange reason, but then she shook it off. They linked arms and laughing they made their way back inside to Nora's party.

"Jack!" Sanjiv shouted bringing him out of his twilight zone.

Having forgotten completely about their upcoming go-cart ride, he turned to look at his new friend meanwhile the two women vanished out of his site.

"Coming!" he yelled back trying to simultaneously search for the two women, but it seemed they had dissipated into thin air. Damn it! He reached Sanjiv just as the go-cart was being prepared for them. They hopped on and throughout the entire ride, Jack's eyes were focused on the last time he saw the women, wondering where they could have gone. He decided he would come back and the next time, he would not let them out of his sight.

"Can we come back? Please mommy?" she had pink colored icing on her left cheek.

'Yes, of course. I had a blast." Fausta exclaimed as she cleaned off her daughter's cheek. She definitely wanted to return.

"Auntie Carly, did you have fun too?"

"Of course!" Carly looked up lovingly at her six-foot four boyfriend. "How about you honey? Would you come back with me?"

He kissed her passionately on the lips. "You bet!"

"Euwwww." Exclaimed Nora.

"Oh, you'll get there one day missy, you'll see."

"Oh no I won't."

"Oh yes you will."

"All right you two, cut it out. Time to go." She turned to Nora. "Did all your friends go home?"

"All except Cynthia. She needs a ride."

"She can come with us. We'll take her home."

"Thanks Carly."

"I'm gonna go find her." Nora ran off.

Carly waited for Nora to be out of sight. "But we're not coming straight home, so don't wait up." Carly winked at her friend.

"Got it." She winked back.

~~~~~~

Jack tossed and turned all night long with a mirage of feelings ranging from love, anger, melancholy, regret, and excitement. He imagined holding Fausta like he did back in Australia when they were dating. What happened? He thought. When did it all go to shit? He thought of the sudden disappearance of her with *his* money. He became angry again and restless, he got up to get some water. When he shut the fridge door, he glared at the small photo of him, and his wife taken only two weeks after they were married in some instant photo booth at the annual fair. The "Greeny Jeanie" in the glass booth told them of the bright future that was ahead of them, the corn dogs, the popcorn, the rides…it was a magical day. "Why did you run away? We were happy, weren't we?" he asked the Fausta smiling back at him in the little photo. He went back to bed but this time he brought the photo with him and as he laid down, he slid the photo under his pillow. Once he was asleep again, his dreams were perturbed and unsettling which awoke him with a feeling of revenge. This feeling changed his ultimate goal from finding his wife and getting back together to finding his wife and getting even.

Chapter 6

Two weeks later, Fausta was at school for a teachers' in-service day. These sessions were unnerving for Fausta because she had to leave Nora home by herself. Nora was ten years old by now and even though she had promised her mother up and down that she would be careful, that uneasy feeling never left Fausta—ever. Every time she came home and found Nora doing her homework, or texting her friends, or watching TV, she took a sigh of relief.

"Okay, let's try it again."

"But mom, I know what to do. Please! Enough now!"

"No! I have to be sure you know what to do. Please. Just once more, and I'll let you go watch your favorite show."

"Fine-a!" she plopped on the couch and crossed her arms in defiant annoyance.

"Right. So, someone knocks at the door, and you don't know who it is. What do you do?"

"I grab the phone, run into my closet, shut the door, and dial 9-1-1." Nora was brooding.

"You missed a step."

"Oh right, I leave the line open."

"Why?"

"So that the cops will come find me if they don't hear anyone on the other end."

"Good girl! Also, because 9-1-1 calls are recorded, so everything the phone picks up gets recorded. Investigators can use those recordings to piece together what happened. Okay, let's try it." Fausta went outside to play a potential robber. She knocked on the door.

"Who is it?" Nora asked like she did a hundred times before.

"It's Brighthouse cable, ma'am."

"Sorry, I can't open the door."

"Good job Nora."

Nora cracked a smile. "I was taught well."

"Okay, so now, there's someone in the house. What do you do?"

"I hide inside the big box that's on the left side of my closet."

"Good, now run and hide. I'm going to time you."

"Sure." She got ready as she always did, standing next to the couch.

"And go!" Fausta clicked the stopwatch.

Nora took off as fast as she could, picked up the phone from the cradle, and headed to her hiding place. Then she shouted "Done!"

Fausta clicked the stopwatch a second time. "Eleven seconds!" she exclaimed, as Nora came back to the living room.

"Great." She commented sarcastically. "Are we done now?" she was itching to get back to texting with her friends.

"Yes, yes, go on." Fausta was annoyed with her daughter. Why couldn't she understand that trouble she could be in? Doesn't she fear for her life?"

"Finally!" Nora was out of her mother's sight faster than a Florida lightning strike.

Fausta rolled her eyes and started dinner.

Later, after Nora had wolfed down her dinner and was in front of the TV watching "Charmed," Fausta sighed again.

"What's wrong?" Carly walked into the room, and immediately sensed Fausta's mood. "You've been huffing and puffing since I got home."

"I'm worried about her. She just doesn't get it."

The wine bottle made a squeaky popping sound as Carly pulled the cork out. She topped off Fausta's glass. "Faussy, she doesn't get it, because she doesn't see the danger." She slid the half-full wine glass towards her friend. "Here, this will help take the edge off."

Fausta nodded, while she drank it like it was a glass of water. "Well, I sure hope she never finds herself in a precarious situation. That would be the death of me!"

"Faussy, he doesn't know we're here." She patted Fausta's hands. "Nobody knows. Remember? We did good, not leaving a trace."

"I know. You're probably right, Carly. But I can't help feeling uneasy when she's at home by herself. My mind races a thousand miles an hour, and I can't help it."

Carly took Fausta's hands in hers and drew them close to herself. "Faussy, I hear you. I do. But you've got to let her be independent. She's ten years old, you know!"

"That's the problem. She's *only* ten!"

"You've raised a very smart girl. Should anything happen, she'll know what to do." She filled her friend's wine glass again. "Now, drink up."

~~~~~~

Jack was at the Melbourne Library, sitting at one of the computer terminals. He didn't have enough money to buy his own, yet, so he used the library. He opened a search engine and typed in Fausta Benito. When he hit enter, nothing showed up.

"Bloody 'ell!" he whispered.

He typed in only "Benito" and found a slew of them— ranging from first names, last names, and business names. But none indicated Fausta.

"Well, shit!" he rubbed his chin and then like a light bulb went off in his head, he typed in Carly McIntyre, Melbourne, Florida and one listing showed up. It was a Myspace account. He clicked on the link and was taken directly to the Myspace log in screen. "You bastard!" This time, he raised his voice a bit. As soon as he noticed people staring at him, he whispered, "Sorry," and hid his face behind the monitor. "Well, I guess it's time to open an account." He created a new My Space account. The site wanted a photo of him, but he didn't have one at the moment. So, he searched for a photo of his favorite Australian actor, Eric Bana, and saved it on the computer. "He looks like me, anyway." He snickered slightly as he used the photo as his avatar. "There I am." He tapped at the photo. "Nice lookin' bloke." Once he received confirmation that his account was active, he searched for Carly. "There she is…wild red curls and all." he scrolled through her page and saw a few photos posted from the night at Andretti's, with a tall fellow. "Huh! I wonder who he is?" Then he read the tagline. *Me and my very handsome PO-PO boyfriend. Jealous ladies?* "Oh, ouch mate, he's a copper," he whispered. He didn't want to mess with local police. He tapped his fingers on the desk and immediately stopped when he noticed dirty looks directed towards him. He rolled his eyes and went to the info tab of her profile page. "Nothin'." He looked at the photo again and squinted and moved closer. "My Faussy took that picture. I know she did." Another idea popped into his noggin at that point. He typed in Fausta Benito, and the answer was No Results Found. "Crickey!" he shouted.

This time one of the female librarians approached. "Sir, I'm going to have to ask you to leave."

"But I…"

"I'm very sorry, sir, but you're disturbing the others."

He looked at her as if to say, *I can take you out right now!'* but he got up, shut down the computer, and left the building. "I'll be back," He bumbled to himself as he mounted his bike. "And I'm going to find an address this time." He began pedaling, as he whistled his favorite tune.

~~~~~~

"Fausta! Look! Look!" Carly waved her left hand in front of Fausta's face.

Fausta displayed a look of shock and amazement. "What?" she pulled her friend's hand closer, so she could get a good look at the ring. "Wow, Carly! I'm so happy for you!" Carly moved her ring finger back and forth so her best friend could see the brilliant sparkle in the Florida sunshine. "Look at that brilliance!"

"I know, right?" Carly still could not believe it. Terrance was the man of her dreams. He had naturally dirty-blonde hair, cut short as required by Melbourne Police Department. His eyes were a piercing blue, that made her melt every time he looked at her in just *that* way. His body was sculptured like the statue of David, except he was probably taller—at least it seemed like that to Carly.

"Come on, let's go inside. I want all the details!"

"Well, you know, I've had a good feeling about him." Carly filled the kettle with cool water and pulled out their special tea that they had ordered from Australia.

"Yes, he's been so wonderful to you. He's polite, sexy—and he treats you like a queen..." Fausta pulled out the tea paraphernalia from their junk drawer. "...which is how you deserve to be treated, obviously."

Carly gave her friend a warm hug. "Aww, you're such a good friend. What would I do without you?"

"Nothing much, I suppose!" They both giggled.

"So, I'm asking you now, before we go any further...will you be my maid of honor?"

Fausta jumped up in delight and clapped her hands. "Yes, of course! of course, I will!"

The kettle began whistling like crazy. Carly removed it from the stove and poured the scalding water into the mugs.

She returned the kettle to the stove and sat back down. "I'm so excited I can hardly breathe."

"I can only imagine." Fausta sighed, replaying her wedding with Jack in her mind's eye. "Ah, I remember those days. So much excitement. Then, so much disappointment." she looked at Carly's frowning face. "Oh, I'm so sorry Carly! I didn't mean to darken the moment."

"It's fine." Carly cracked a smile.

"All right, then." Fausta inhaled. "When is the wedding?"

That question sparked an instantaneous change of mood. "How about a Christmas wedding?"

"Oh, I love Christmas! That's a brilliant idea!"

As the women finished their tea and discussed wedding plans, Nora sauntered in.

"Nora, can you come here, please?"

"Sure Mom." Seconds later, she was standing front and center, peering at the two women. "What's going on?" she knew something was up.

"Oh, nothing much," Carly said, waving her left hand in front of Nora's face. "Just getting married, is all."

Nora let out a screech. "Wow, Auntie Carly, this is beautiful!" she peered at her again. "Wait. You're marrying Terry, right?"

"Of course, silly. Who else?"

It was Nora's turn, now, to clap her hands in delight, as she hopped up and down. Then all three joined hands and did a sort of *Ring Around the Rosie* dance. Except, it wasn't about death. It was about new life.

~~~~~~

Early in the morning the next Saturday, Fausta was preparing Nora's favorite breakfast: French toast. "Nora! Breakfast!"

"Coming, Mom!" Still in her jammies, she went to her usual seat at the breakfast nook. "Where's Auntie Carly?"

"She's with Terry." She dished out the toast.

"Oh, okay." She quickly devoured one of the toasts.

"Slow down, young lady. It's not proper for a young lady to wolf her food down like that." She raised an eyebrow.

"Well, I'm hungry so…" she took another huge bite.

"All right, good. So, what do you want to do today?" she asked this rhetorical question, because she knew well what her daughter wanted to do.

"Disney World?" she asked as she cleaned her plate.

"Yes."

"Yes? Really?"

"Yes but…"

"Oh, here it comes…but?"

"I want your room spotless."

"Oh, is that it?" she picked up her plate and placed it in the sink. "Yes, I can do that." She shot out of sight and disappeared into her room.

Smiling, Fausta shook her head. At ten years old, her daughter knew well how to get what she wanted. She was going to be a clever young woman one day. "I don't want her to grow up, please?" she spoke to a photo of the Merciful Redeemer that was hanging on her kitchen wall, right next to the calendar.

Jack arrived at the house. There was only one car parked in the driveway, so he figured it would be either Fausta's or Carly's. He looked around to see if anyone was around. Then he made his way to the back. Through the kitchen sliding door, he heard nothing. But he saw Fausta in the kitchen with a set of earbuds plugged into a cell phone tucked inside her apron pocket. When he knocked lightly and saw that she didn't move, he forced the sliding door open and slid in. She was at the sink, so he snuck up on her. He grabbed her waist with a tight grip and spun her around rapidly.

"G'day, darlin'. Well blow me down! Finally found ya, slag!" he wrapped his right hand around her neck. "Did ya think I was a galan? Did ya?" he shouted as he pushed her to the floor.

"Jack!" she yelled loudly so Nora could hear. "Get out, Jack! Get out! Now!" She was shocked! She could not believe what she saw. *How in hell did he find me?*

"Ya skanky ho'! I aint goin' anywhere without my dough." He tightened his grip. "Where is it?" he slapped her with his left hand, but she didn't move because of his grip. "Huh? Where is it?" he slapped her again, making her lip bleed.

Nora ran into her bedroom, grabbing the phone, just as she was taught. And, just as she was taught, she hid inside the designated place. She dialed 9-1-1 and did not say a word, like she had practiced for what had seemed like a thousand times. She knew that the police would come if she stayed silent. She was terrified and she trembled. But she stayed quiet as a church mouse. Her bedroom door was open, and she heard everything clearly.

"I don't have it, Jack. I spent it on this house."

Jack looked around. "You blew my dough on this 'ouse?"

She nodded the best that she could. Her eyes were bulging from her sockets. But he didn't relax his grip.

Shit! he was thinking. "Bloody 'ell!" he pulled her to the first bedroom he found, which turned out to be Nora's. "Well, if I can't get my dough, then a pash-rash will have to do, won't it?" Releasing her, he threw her on the bed. With his back to the closet, he undid his belt and his zipper.

"No, Jack, no! Please! I'll give you the money! Please, Jack, please!" she was horrified at the thought of Nora being in the closet.

"Shut up! Just shut up! You whore! You stole my money, left me, and ran to this shitty town!" Holding her down, he climbed on top of her. He wrapped his hands tightly around her neck. "Why did you leave me? Why did you steal my money?" he tightened his grip, even more, as she fought to breathe. "Why Faussy? Why?" As he clinched tighter, she gasped for air.

"Mmmm, huh, ahhh…" Her arms and legs flailed, uselessly. She fought as hard as she could to loosen his constricting fingers around her neck.

"Tell me why, Faussy! Why? I loved you! We could have been so happy together." Suddenly he let her go. She gasped in some precious air.

Still on the bed, Fausta moved away from Jack and positioned herself at the opposite edge of the bed. "Jack, please, let me make you some tea and let's talk. Please!" she pleaded with him. But when she saw him pull out a piece of white nylon cord, she panicked. "No! Jack! No!" she yelled.

Jack slowly approached her with that devious look and hooked the rope around her neck. He pulled the two ends as tight as he could, until she no longer fought back. "Why did you leave me? Why did you come here? Now, look what you made me do! Just look at ya!" He looked at his hands still holding the rope and stunned to see the motionless body of his wife. He started bawling. "Damn it, woman! Now what?" He realized that he couldn't leave her there, so he lifted her body and heaved it over his shoulder. Still in tears, he shouted to her lifeless body; "See what you've made me do? I had no choice." He walked out the way he came in, with Fausta on his shoulder. He sat her on one of the patio chairs. His initial intention was to leave her there. But then he had an idea. He went to the front, hopped into his Ford Ranger, and drove it to the backyard which was not fenced. He got out, opened the tailgate, heaved his wife's body into the truck bed, covered her with blue tarp that he kept in his truck, closed the tailgate, and drove off. He searched around for nosy neighbors but oddly enough, there was nobody around at that hour of the afternoon. "Where am I going to put 'er?" he asked himself out loud as he drove. Killing her had not been his intent, but now he had to find somewhere to   bury   her.   But   where?

Chapter 7

Nora was frozen. Still hiding inside her closet and having heard the entire ordeal, she was in extreme shock. She heard sirens, and a few minutes later she heard male voices shouting gibberish. When the Melbourne police officer came into her room and opened the closet door pointing his pistol at her, she shrieked. He found her with both her hands covering her face, in the fetal position, the phone tucked under her leg, face down—still connected to 9-1-1.

He holstered his weapon. "Miss? Did you call? Miss?" he reached out his hand, but she didn't move a muscle. "2190 to Melbourne. We have a child hidden in a closet," he spoke into his radio's microphone.

He again addressed Nora. "Miss, please come out. We'd like to speak to you. Please." he extended his hand a second time.

Nora shook her head and hid her face again.

"2190 to Melbourne."

"Go ahead, 2190."

"We need a female officer here. The young girl is terrified and won't come out of the closet."

"Ten-four, 2190. Sending a female officer your way."

"Okay little girl, I'm staying right here until you come out. Nothing is going to happen to you."

Then there were some familiar voices.

"Please! Let me in! She's my best friend! Please! I live here! This is my home! Please!" Carly tried to push past the two officers guarding the door.

Terrance pulled out his badge and flashed it to both officers. "She's my fiancée, and I can attest that she lives here."

"My ten-year-old niece is in there! I can help!" Carly pushed her way in and headed straight for Nora's room. "Nora!"

"Auntie Carly!" she fell into Carly's warm and familiar arms.

"Oh, baby, oh baby!" she cuddled and rocked her, holding as tight as she could. "What happened?"

Nora couldn't talk. She hid her face in Carly's bosom and sobbed. Carly tried to set her on the bed, but Nora cried out, "No! Not there! No!" she loosened her embrace and ran into Fausta's room.

Carly followed her. "I'm sorry, Nora. Where's your mum?" she was terrified that her horrible suspicion would be confirmed by the young girl.

"Jack. He took her." She climbed on her mother's bed and got into the fetal position again. This time, she was rocking back and forth.

"Jack?" horrified, she blinked and sat next to Nora. "H-he was h-here?"

"Yes! And he took her!"

"He took her? Where?"

"I don't know! I didn't see anything. I only heard his voice." She hugged her aunt again. But this time the crying was louder and more terrifying.

"I hid in the closet, just as Mommy told me to. I couldn't see anything, 'cuz the openings in the doors are too small. All I could see was his back! But I heard him! He was yelling something about money. Mom said that she had used it to buy the house. Jack got real mad at that. He brought her in my room and threw her on the bed. He kept yelling at her. Louder and louder. She was making funny noises, like she couldn't breathe. I heard her say, 'No, Jack, no.' And then she started making these horrible noises again. Like gurgling sounds. Then she stopped talking. I heard him say, 'See what you've made me do? I had no choice.' He said that as he was leaving the room."

At that, the officers corded off the bedroom with yellow crime scene tape. They also made everyone leave the house, so as not to contaminate the scene any more than it already was.

"2190 to Melbourne."

"2190," came the monotonic reply.

"I'm going to need CSI and a detective out here. We have an abduction and possible homicide."

"Ten-four, 2190. Melbourne to CSI-1."

"CSI-1, go ahead.

"Respond to 2190's location reference abduction and possible homicide."

"Ten-four. Enroute."

In due time, Detectives Roth Sabbath and Matthew Simmons showed up, followed by CSI investigator Sabine Santos. Roth and Matt were both seasoned detectives. Roth was a large man, standing six feet four inches, with a hefty build, dark curly brown hair trimmed military-style. He had sparkling emerald eyes but, in this situation, they were fogged with anger over a woman that could be missing or dead under his watch. He had been on the department for twenty years and had seen just about as much of this garbage as he could stand. He was counting down the time until he could retire.

Matt was a much smaller man, five feet nine inches, with straight blonde hair in a military-style buzz cut. He sported a thin mustache. He, too, was muscular, with his biceps filling his short shirt sleeves. He had only ten years' experience but had spent ten years in the Air Force OSI. He was well-rounded, experience-wise.

Sabine was a slender twenty-something. She had flaming red hair with a touch of blue highlight, that she kept short. In her line of work, it wasn't absolutely necessary, but she figured it would be easier to manage, to prevent cross-contamination. Sabine was newly trained. She knew the basics of evidence collection and had been through the field training program. She definitely knew her job.

"Hey Matt, who's the new CSI?" asked Roth.

"Dunno. Sabine, I think. I've heard of her. She's done pretty well in smaller things: criminal mischief, burglaries, that sort of thing. I don't think she's done any major case work. Probably ought to keep an eye on her."

Actually, this was Sabine's first major case. She was relishing it and, of course, wanted to prove herself among the "big boys." Sabine went to work. She put on her personal protective suit and booties to prevent contaminating the scene.

She took photos of the room. First, from the doorway, then from inside—from all angles. The bed had been made that morning, and Sabine clearly saw the outline where a struggle had taken place. She closely examined the bed and found several hairs about halfway up. They were dark hairs, long, and somewhat wavy. She took several photographs—first from a slight distance with evidence markers, and then closer in to show the detail. She took the hairs, placing each one in a small envelope, and marking the envelope with the case number and the precise location discovered. She knew she had to do this one "by the book," because it likely would prove to be a complicated case.

As she continued to visually scour the bed, she came across some shorter hairs, dark, but quite different in appearance from the others. "Hey, guys, come look at this!"

"Watcha got?" came the reply from Roth.

"Hairs. Different from the ones I got from up here. Look. They could be what the vic pulled from the perp during the struggle."

"Hey, good catch! Bag 'em."

"Already on it!" Sabine was busy collecting the new hair samples. Roth and Matt exchanged knowing glances.

Once Sabine and the detectives were satisfied that they had collected everything from the bed, Sabine brought out the ultraviolet light.

Matt looked at her, quizzically. "What're you doing? She wasn't killed here."

"You do your job; I'll do mine," came the quick reply.

"Whoa! Sorry for stepping on your toes!"

"No problem. Sorry for snapping at you. I just want to make sure I catch everything. As you know, once we leave here, we're through. There's no coming back."

"Fair enough," said Matt. "Carry on."

Sabine turned out the lights in the bedroom. The blinds were drawn and darkened the room somewhat, but not entirely. She illuminated the bed first, hoping to find body fluids: blood, semen, something. She struck out.

She then turned her attention to the floor. It was covered with a light-colored Berber carpet with small, multicolored spots imprinted in the fabric. *Holy cow! I don't think I'll **ever** find anything on this carpet!* However, she went through the motions, anyway. At least, she would put on a good show for these seasoned detectives.

Matt pulled Roth aside, out of the room, and out of earshot. "What the hell does she think she's going to find on *this* carpet?"

"For the life of me, I don't know. Well, you know these newbies. Got to make it look good."

"Yeah, you're right. And who knows, she might find something."

"Not likely, but okay."

"Hey! Come look at this!" The shout startled both of them. They hurried back into the room.

"What?" said Matt.

She pointed to a purple-illuminated spot on the carpet.

"What?" said Roth. "I don't see anything."

"Sabina pointed. "Look. Right here."

The two men looked closer. Roth suddenly said, "Yup. I see it!"

"Where?"

"Right there, Matt. See?"

"Oh, yeah. Wow, that's a tiny drop, Sabine. I'll hold the light if you want to shoot some photos."

"Yeah, I have to take a measurement first. Hold on."

She used the theodolite to precisely locate the droplet on the crime scene diagram. Then she shot photos. The same process as before: from the door with a marker, and then up close. Finally, with Matt holding the light, she very carefully snipped the sample out of the carpet, placed it inside an evidence envelope, and marked and sealed it.

Finally, "Well, guys, I think I'm done in this room. Is there anything else you can think of for me to do? Otherwise, I'm going to look elsewhere in the house."

"No, Sabine. I think you have everything," said Matt. "Thanks for your help, and excellent find with the light."

Roth piped up, "Right-o. You can work scenes with us, any time!"

"You got that right. You've certainly proven yourself today," added Matt.

"Hey, thanks, guys. I really appreciate that." Sabine took her bags of evidence out to her van, where she secured them.

Terrance took Roth aside. "Hey, listen. I'm Carly's fiancé and I knew the victim well. She was Carly's best friend. I mean they were like two sisters. Nora in there called Carly her auntie."

"I see. So, do you want to assist with this case? Or do you want to stay out of it?" he pulled out his notepad and scribbled.

"Oh, I want to assist. We need to find Fausta and quick."

"Yes, the first 48 hours are the most important in any abduction."

Terrance looked at Nora and shook his head. "God, she's in terrible shape. I can't even fathom going through what she just went through."

"So, tell me, do you know who this Jack guy is?" he opened his small notebook.

"Yes, he's Fausta's husband."

"Husband?" he scribbled.

"Yeah. Story goes that when Fausta found out she was pregnant, she left Australia with Carly to start a new life and give Nora a chance at a peaceful life."

"Why is that?"

"Because he was abusive. Very abusive, according to Carly. Fausta was afraid that Jack might do the same to Nora, so she took her friend's advice and fled to Florida."

"When did all this happen?"

"Well, Nora just celebrated her tenth birthday, I'd say about three weeks ago. So, maybe around 1998?"

He scribbled some more. "Okay, that'll do for now. I'll call you if CSI comes up with anything. She found some hair and a bit of body fluid. We're hoping that something comes of it."

Terrance nodded.

"Oh, and I'm really sorry for your loss."

"It's not me I'm worried about; it's Nora."

He slowly walked into Fausta's room to find Nora in the arms of Carly, sobbing quietly. His heart sank. "Hey honey, we have to leave."

"Leave? Why?" Carly asked.

"CSI needs to conduct a thorough investigation and you can't be here while they do that."

"Did you hear that, Nora?" Carly tried to free herself from Nora. "We've got to go honey." She got off the bed and slowly pulled Nora off as well. "Come, I'll help you pack." She looked at Terrance. "We're going to stay with Terry for a few days. Would you like that?"

Terrance nodded and cracked a smile.

"Can I play with Scoot?"

Scoot was Terrance's miniature Dachshund. "You bet. You know how he loves to play with you."

Nora released her grip on Carly and shook her head. "I'm not going in there," pointing to her room.

"Oh, don't worry, I'll get your things. You stay here, okay?" Carly didn't waste any time. She wanted to get Nora out of there as soon as possible. Even she couldn't process what had just happened to her best friend.

Terrance interrupted. "No, you two have to leave immediately. You can't wander through the house until CSI gets done. It really could hurt whatever case we end up making against Jack—or whomever.

"Okay, I'll get the car started," Carly interjected.

"I'll stay with you." Terrance sat down on the edge of the bed and Nora sat in his lap. "Is that okay?"

"Yes." Still very shaky, she sank into his arms.

Terrance was very attentive not to damage this terrified little creature with his strong arms. He held her as tight as possible without pressure. "Can I ask you a question about your mom?"

"Y-yes…" she whispered.

"Did you see what he did to your mom?"

He felt her nod while in his embrace.

"He-he pulled his pants down."

Terrance knew exactly what that was, but he restrained himself. "Did he say anything while he did that?"

She didn't answer right away but after a short while she separated from his embrace and looked him in the eyes. "Ummm…something about stealing his money…then he called her a whore…then…she was crying…then…she wasn't talking anymore."

"What do you mean by that, Nora?"

"He kept talking but mom didn't answer."

"Okay so could it be that he had his hand over her mouth to silence her?"

"Maybe."

"Okay, and then what?"

"Then he took her and put her over his shoulders. Her arms just dangled."

"Did your mom say anything or do anything?"

"N-no…she was quiet…she knew I was in the closet…why didn't she look at me?"

"She knew you were there?"

"Yes. We practiced it many times."

"What do you mean practiced?"

Carly walked into the bedroom. "Ready? Let's go."

Terrance picked up Nora and carried her out of the house and into his Explorer. He buckled her in and signaled to Carly to sit in the back next to her. He got into the driver seat and fired up the engine.

"Nora, are you okay? Are you hungry?"

"No Auntie, I'm not hungry. Can we just go home? I want to play with Scoot."

"Sure kiddo, home it is." Terrance drove quietly as he contemplated what he had just heard from Nora. *What about the money? How was Fausta still married? Didn't she divorce before she left Australia?* He would have to ask Carly as soon as Nora went to sleep.

"She didn't touch her food."

"Carly, do you really expect her to eat after what she's been through?"

"I suppose not." She looked at Scoot and thought how lucky dogs were to never know what real problems are.

"Carly, I need to ask you some questions."

For some strange reason, she could not take her eyes off Scoot. He was squeaking his favorite squeaky toy, a striped monkey. He would go on for minutes without stopping. Didn't he know? What was he thinking?

"Earth to Carly…"

She blinked a few times. "Yes, yes, I'm here." She looked at her fiancé's face. How excited she had been over the last couple of weeks; planning a wedding with her best friend, and now she was gone. "I can't believe she's gone."

"That's not necessarily so."

"What do you mean?"

"I mean, she's missing, yes, but it doesn't mean she's dead."

"What? Of course, she is. Didn't you hear Nora?" she couldn't believe he actually believed that.

He gently moved her face so he could look into her eyes. "Carly, we didn't find a body and there's no blood. So, it could be that she's gone missing but still alive."

"Are you serious? You think she's alive?"

"She could be." He smiled at his fiancée. "Until there's evidence of a death, there is hope."

Carly rested her head on Terrance's virile chest and wept softly. He didn't move, but just held her as tightly as he could while gently stroking her wild red hair. When she was ready, she took a deep breath, wiped her eyes, and smiled at Terrance. "Okay, I'll pack some things and we'll go to a hotel."

"Why go to a hotel? Just come stay with me. I have plenty of room."

"Really?"

"Of course, Carly. I wouldn't have it any other way."

Carly turned to a noticeably quiet Nora and crouched down. "Honeybun, can you make me a list of what you need?"

With a passive look on her face, she nodded.

Carly hugged the girl but didn't feel any response. Her heart broke for Nora. *What an awful way to lose your mother! Will she ever recover?* It already looked like she had an arduous job ahead of her, having to be an adoptive parent, a psychologist, a confidant, and just a friend—on top of grieving for her best friend, who truly was the only sister she ever had. She held Nora a little while longer, and when she let go, she said, "Hey Honeybun, you know I'm here for you, right? I promise you; they will find your mom."

Another weak nod.

Carly picked up a pad and a pencil and handed them to Nora. "Here you go."

Nora took both items and began writing.

~~~~~~

"Do you think he killed her?"

"There's a good chance." Detective Sabbath stared at his computer monitor.

"Honestly, I have to disagree. There was no blood and her daughter only supposedly saw a rape, she didn't see a killing."

"Yes, but she saw her lifeless mother being carried off. This could mean she was dead when he hauled her off."

"Still doesn't mean anything. He could have just knocked her out and taken her away. He may have kidnapped her to take her to a hiding place."

"Or take her back to Australia."

Terrance's eyebrows raised in astonishment. "I'm calling all Florida airport authorities to block any flights to Australia."

"Yep, tell them that every plane needs to be inspected before it takes off."

"I'll tell them to look for a man and a woman in their early forties that matches the descriptions of them."

Within the next twenty-four hours, a color photo of Fausta was all over the news networks and the online news websites as well. He set up a toll-free number that was advertised, along with her photo, so any person living in Florida would be able to call with any tips or information. Within the next several days, Detective Sabbath set up a statewide search for Fausta Benito. He had posters printed, along with lawn signs that got posted in all police stations and Sherriff departments, in color, so she would be easily recognized. The lawn signs were given to every Space Coast resident that they could reach. It looked like election season, even though the national elections were far away. This massive undertaking was missing one crucial thing: a photo of Jack. Detective Sabbath called the Australian authorities requesting a photo of this man, but it seemed he was a needle in a haystack located Down Under. After three days of unsuccessfully calling the overseas authorities, Terrance's patience was dwindling.

~~~~~~

Jack went about his usual business and kept his life as normal as possible, doing his best to not raise any suspicions. When he hopped into his truck, the stench was strong enough to make him hurl. "I've got to find a place for ya, darlin'. But where?" He never wanted to kill his wife; he had let his emotions get the best of him—along with his strength, which had increased dramatically, due to his daily workouts at the F.I.T. gym, to which he had access any time of the day or night.

"I've got to get rid of ya, but where?" For three days he had been searching for a proper burial place, while asking himself the same question. He had purchased a shovel and a pick in two different hardware stores, again to not invite any scrutiny, whatsoever.

There was a big shindig going on in Downtown Melbourne for Labor Day, and amongst the various vendors was a murder-mystery author. Jack somehow gravitated there while carrying his dark beer.

"Hey buddy, do you like murder-mystery books?" John Max called out, as Jack approached his table. He was middle-aged, bushy mustachioed man with slim build, dressed in jeans and a green t-shirt that said, *'I Labor Every day!'*

"Yeah, I do mate." But he *did* murders, not *read about* them.

"Oh, down under, eh?" the author asked as he slid his fingers through his salt-and-pepper hair.

"Yeah, mate." He picked up one of his books and turned it over to read the blurb.

"That book is set in this area in the early fifties."

"Oh?"

"Yeah, so, do you like murder stories?" John Max asked.

"Oh yeah, I find them fascinatin'." He gave the book to John. "I'll take it."

"Oh, cool." John was a seasoned author who lived in Satellite Beach and sold his books in person only. He was old school and didn't like this new e-book business. He loathed modern technology.

"I have a question for ya, mate."

"Shoot." He signed the book. "Who am I signing it for?"

"Faussy. She's my wife."

"Okay. This book is to die for. Tell her that."

"Oh, I will." He grinned.

"So, how do you spell it?"

"F-A-U-S-S-Y."

"Got it." He wrote her name, slipped a bookmark inside, and handed it to Jack. "So, what's your question?"

"If you had a dead body, where would you hide it?"

The author laughed loudly. "Ha-ha! I get that question all the time."

"Ya do, eh?"

"Yeah." He tapped his chin. "Well, there are several good places that I've used in my books, but the best place is Three Forks—it's swampy and has plenty of gators and other scavengers to dispose of the body."

"I see." Jack shuddered. He did not want his wife to become alligator food. That would be too gruesome. "What about without those gators?"

"No gators, eh? Okay…how about the Compound then?"

"The Compound? What's that?"

"It's in southwest Palm Bay, in the middle of nowhere. Perfect place for a clean burial."

"Hey that's cool, mate. Seeya soon." He gave the author his money, thinking his advice alone was worth every penny.

"Compound. Compound." He said the word repeatedly, as he headed for his truck, finishing his dark beer. He unlocked his truck, which was parked a good distance away from other cars, so the "fragrance" would go unnoticed. He threw the book on the back seat and took off. A few miles down the road, he stopped at a 7-Eleven to gas up. He noticed some Hibiscus plants, of all different colors, lined up at the front of the store. *Huh*, He silently commented as he headed inside. "Hey mate, are those plants out there for sale?"

"Yeah man." The brown-haired, blue-eyed, young man, with a piercing coming out of his nose answered. He proudly wore an F.I.T. hoodie with a 7-Eleven badge that read ,"Mitch".

"How much are they?"

The young man pulled out a clipboard. "Ummmm, five dollars, man."

"Right. I'll take them all. Mum loves those plants."

The college kid smiled and rang them up. "That's thirty dollars, man."

Jack pulled out the exact change. "Here ya go, but I got a question for ya."

"Sure man, what do you need to know?" he placed the cash in the register.

"I've got to go to the Compound. Do you know where it is?"

"Oh yeah, man, we go there all the time to shoot."

"Oh yeah?"

"Yeah, it's pretty popular to go shoot your weapons where nobody bothers you. Especially cops."

Jack grinned at that comment. He always hated coppers. "Can you give me directions?"

"I'll do ya one better. Here, I'll draw ya a map." He pulled out a steno pad and began drawing a map with his pencil. "Here. This is pretty straightforward. You can't go wrong."

"Hey thanks, mate." He gently folded the map and slid it in the front pocket of his jeans. "See ya." And left.

Per the map, he drove south down Babcock Street until he reached Malabar Road, where he turned right. While he drove, he laid the map on his lap, to make sure he was going the right way, while he blasted another of his favorite tunes, *Won't Get fooled again,* by The Who.

When he reached Minton Road, he made a left, then a right on Jupiter Boulevard, and then a quick left onto DeGroodt Road. When he reached Bayside Lakes Boulevard, he stopped at the red light and pulled out his map. "Where is Bombardier?" Then he noticed the street sign had two different street names: Bayside Lakes Blvd to the left and

Bombardier to the right. "Right it is." He drove about four miles, made a few curves, until there was no road left. He got out of his truck, leaving the high beams on, and scrutinized the area to make sure there was nobody around. "Perfect," he said, as he went to the back to pull out his pick and shovel. Suddenly, he stopped dead in his tracks. He saw a bunch of shotgun shells in the cul-de-sac and remembered the words of the kid at the 7-Eleven: *Yeah, it's pretty popular to go shoot your weapons.* Jack suddenly realized that even though the coppers might not be out here, a lot of other folks came here. He had to find another site.

Jack got back into his truck, swearing under his breath. This effort had taken on a life of its own. He drove back about a mile and turned onto another road. He had absolutely no idea where he was because there were no street signs. There were no stop signs. There were no signs, whatsoever. *Crickey, this place gives me the freakin' heebie-jeebies!* After a few more turns, he was where he figured no one would be likely to go. He stopped the truck, again, and pulled out his tools. He dug, and dug for what seemed like hours, quietly making a shallow grave. Then he hauled his wife's dead body, wrapped in a rug that he had found in the trash at the complex where he lived, effortlessly toward the grave. He breathed through his mouth instead of his nose so he wouldn't gag. However, the stench was still overwhelming.

He threw Fausta in the grave, tucking her in gently, as he wanted her, in some twisted act of compassion, to be as comfortable as possible. "You should be good here, Love." He began shoveling dirt over her body until she was completely covered. Once he was done with the shoveling, he planted the Hibiscus plants on her grave, so he could find it when he came to visit later. He then covered the grave with palm fronds. "There. Nobody will find you 'ere, love." He smiled and clapped his hands to rid them of the dirt. Just before he got back into his truck, something came over him. He dropped to his knees. "Lord, I'm so sorry about this. But please let her not be found, so that she can rest in peace. I'm sorry, love. I really didn't want it to end up like this. I'm sorry...I'm sorry..." tears streamed down his sculpted cheeks as he got in his truck and drove off.

Chapter 8

For the first six months or so, the Melbourne Police Department received a flurry of leads ranging from people who had seen either Fausta or Jack, or both of them together. After more than six months of continually checking each and every lead, the tips slowly began to dwindle, along with any hope of ever finding Fausta.

Even the Australian authorities sent Detective Sabbath the case file about Giacomo Rinaldi, AKA Jack, and the killing of Jessica Richards. The file contained all the notes taken by the two inspectors at that time, photos of the crime scene, along with his incarceration reports, the original charge that landed him in jail, and a photo of a very young and handsome Jack on his wedding day. There also was another photo, taken upon his release from prison. Both detectives, along with Terrance, noticed the huge difference between the two photos of Jack. One depicted a joyous and innocent looking young man with a smile that could melt any heart; the other showed an angry, malicious, and weathered thirty-year-old with anger noticeably lodged deep within his eyes.

Not only did those six months take a toll on the investigation, but also on Carly. Over time, she became irritable, anxious, fatigued, and extremely depressed. She had difficulties focusing on her job. She had problems sleeping, constant mood swings, and she was losing weight at an alarming rate. She even moved the wedding day to the next year. Terrance was frightened, to say the least, and didn't know how to handle the delicate situation. He had a pitiful feeling in his gut that he would not be marrying the love of his life.

Nora also manifested symptoms of post-traumatic stress. She became irritable, just like Carly. She became defiant at home and began bullying other children at school. She became sullen and withdrawn. She rarely went outdoors and got almost no exercise. She began gaining weight and became rather chubby. Carly sent Nora to a child psychologist, Dr. Kristen Johnson, who assisted the girl through the stages of grief. One of the first things that Dr. Johnson suggested was to severely limit Nora's access to television, radio, and the internet. Nora was encouraged to read and do other activities like learning music or trying out for a sport. Nora did both. She learned how to play piano and she signed up for the Melbourne Youth Soccer League. Initially, she was withdrawn and stayed by herself. But fortunately, she had a coach that knew a bit about her story.

Coach Ralph was a big, Italian man, in his middle thirties. He looked imposing at first, but when he began to speak, he came across as a big, teddy bear. However, he took no guff from anyone—players, parents, or referees. He forced Nora to participate. "No 'bench-potatoes' on my team," he was wont to say. With Coach Ralph's encouragement, Nora slowly became more participatory. She dropped the attitude and began making new friends. After six months, she still had nightmares. But they were becoming fewer and farther between, and to Terrance she seemed to be coping better than Carly—especially since she had witnessed the abduction.

"How did your session go today, honeybun?"

"It was okay. You know, the usual." She threw her backpack over the stool back. "What about you Auntie Carly?" Nora knew well that her aunt was struggling much more than she was. She had noticed many changes, but the most drastic was when Carly told her she didn't want to marry Terrance anymore.

"Oh, I'm okay." Carly sighed.

"Auntie Carly, why are you doing this to yourself? You've got to snap out of it. You've got to start living again and reconsider marrying Terry!" The youngster noticed the quick glint of moisture glisten her aunt's emerald eyes. That was about all that was bright about Carly lately.

"I can't...I just can't...look at me, Nora!" she motioned her hand over her body, "How can I marry Terry looking like this? I'm hideous. He doesn't want me anymore." Carly ran off to her room.

Terrance and Carly weren't even sleeping together anymore. What was the point? He didn't want her. He was vibrant, virile, healthy and sexual. She was thin, sickly, her hair was falling out by the bunches, and she could hardly concentrate. She had taken a leave of absence and time was running out. She knew well she had to do something. But what?

When Terrance got home, he found Nora in the backyard practicing her dribbling and kicking.

"Hey honeybun."

She looked up at him and ran into his arms. "Uncle Terry, you've got to do something about her. She is getting worse. Please help her, please!" she pleaded.

Terrance hugged her tight, closed his eyes, and prepared himself mentally for another battle. These were becoming more frequent, and he was wearing out. Not only did the investigation seem at a dead end, but Carly's mental condition was becoming very grave. An intervention was truly needed. "Yes, it's time." He put Nora down. "Come on, I need your help."

They walked in through the kitchen sliding door and headed to Carly's room. Terrance entered first to find Carly sprawled across the bed, and what seemed like dozens of white pills all over the carpet.

"What the…" Terrance quickly checked her neck for a pulse. "She's breathing." He took her lifeless body into his arms. "Nora! Call 9-1-1! Now!"

Nora did not have to be told twice. She picked up the phone that was in the family room and dialed the emergency number.

"9-1-1, what is your emergency?"

"It's my aunt, she's not breathing…" she heard Terrance call her from the bedroom.

"Bring me the phone, Nora!"

She didn't hesitate.

"Hey this is Terrance Bouchuroix, ID 2190. Please send an ambulance 10-18. My fiancée seems to have taken barbiturates and is barely breathing. Please hurry." He was strangely calm. His police instincts were taking over, allowing him to be calm and collected.

Seven minutes later, the ambulance arrived, along with a police cruiser and Detective Sabbath who heard the call on his two-way radio. The ambulance crew worked Carly and got her on a respirator with oxygen and loaded her into the ambulance.

"I'm coming." Terrance stated as he hopped on the ambulance and sat next to Carly. "Can you watch Nora, please?"

"Sure, I got this. Take care of Carly, ya hear?"

"I will. Thanks." And the ambulance doors were slammed shut. Sirens and lights were blazing as the vehicle took off towards Holmes Medical Center.

A terrified Nora was standing on the front porch, staring at the ambulance. Detective Sabbath sat in one of the Muskoka chairs. "Come, sit."

Nora sat on his lap. "Is she going to die, too?"

"No, Nora, she's okay. She just needs some medical attention. Terrance is with her. She's going to be fine. I promise."

"Are you sure?"

"Yes. I promise and I always keep my promises."

~~~~~~

In agreement with the specialist, Terrance took a break from work to care for Carly. He did not want to lose the love of his life and he was willing to do anything to help her. Dr. Osbourne knew well that Carly McIntyre was in deep depression, the natural result of blaming herself for the disappearance of her best friend. It was going to be an arduous task to convince her otherwise, but she was up for the challenge—as long as Terrance was on her playing field.

The treatment plan took a good eight months to complete, and when Carly was strong enough to go back to work, so did Terrance. As she got back to a somewhat normal life, their relationship was far from it. Something broke when Carly attempted suicide, and he couldn't quite put his finger on it. He too, had several sessions with Dr. Osbourne.

"What am I doing wrong, Doc?" he asked.

"Terrance, you need to have patience." He looked up at the police officer over his readers and smiled.

The psychiatrist's dark face with darker freckles made Terrance feel at ease. There was something very familiar about Dr. Osbourne, like he was a family member or that grandfather figure he never had. His voice was warm, yet firm.

"If you say so, Doc."

A few months later, Terrance thought it was time again to address their wedding. Even after the assurances by Dr. Osbourne, he still felt like she was drifting away.

"Hey honey, I'm taking you out tonight."

"Where?" she asked curtly.

"To Lakeside Bistrò."

"Sure, okay." She was in the mood for a nice dinner, but Lakeside Bistrò was very expensive and that meant he had something important to talk about. She had a good idea what it was.

"Great." His voice gave it all away.

"On second thought, no."

"No? Why?"

"Terry, I know what you want, and the answer is no. I'm sorry, I don't want to talk over the phone, but I really don't want to commit to anything."

He was getting nervous. He didn't like where this was going. "It's okay Carly, we can talk about commitments later on, right now, let's just have a quiet dinner."

"I've got to get back. I'll see you at home later on. Bye."

The phone went dead. Terrance felt gnawing at the pit of his stomach. He shook his head.

Carly walked in around nine. "Hey there."

"Carly, please sit." He was seriously upset.

"Not now, Terry…"

"Yes, now! Sit!"

That angry tone stopped her in her tracks. She sat down, placing her handbag on her lap.

"Carly, I want to marry you, now more than ever. Let's set a date, please. I can't keep second guessing when you want to settle down." He pulled his phone out. "Come on, let's set a date tonight." He pulled up his calendar.

Carly sighed. "No Terrance, I don't want to get married."

"But why? Don't you love me?"

"Yes, I do. I can't explain why I don't want to get married, I just don't, and nothing you say will change my mind."

Shocked, Terrance stood there staring at her. "What do you want to do, then? I need some kind of commitment from you. I can't go on like this."

"Fine then. Nora and I will go back home. I've got to get the tenants out first, but if that's what you want…"

"You still haven't told me why." Deep down he was terrified to know the reason.

"I just can't marry you Terry, nor anyone else for that matter. I'm the only one responsible for Nora and I need to dedicate my energy to her. I need to provide for her, and I need to keep a roof over her head. I've got to continue where Fausta left off, and I need to do it alone."

He peered at her then threw his hands in the air. "Fine! Have it your way! Leave me. Go ahead. Leave the only person who will ever love you. You'll never find another guy like me. Never."

Carly didn't move. "I know Terry, I know. But I have to do this, and I have to do it alone." She got up. "I'm going to tell Nora."

Terrance plopped on the couch saddened by what he just heard. He covered his face with his hands. "What have I done?"

Carly knocked on Nora's door but got no answer. She opened it to find her ear buds on while she was on her laptop surfing the net.

"Hey honeybun."

Nora looked up at her aunt. She didn't like the look on her face. She removed her earbuds and shut the laptop. "What's up?"

"We need to talk."

"Okay?"

"We're moving out?"

Nora sat up straight. "Moving out! Where?"

"We're going back home."

"Back there? But why?" she frowned.

"We have to, because we can't stay here any longer."

"Are you breaking up with Uncle Terry?"

"Yes, honeybun."

Tears welled in Nora's eyes. "But, why?"

Carly turned to face Nora. "Because I made a promise to your mom and Terry isn't part of it. That's why."

"I-I don't understand. You can both take care of me. We could be a family. Please, Auntie Carly. Don't do this. Please!"

"No honeybun, I have to. I owe it to your mom, and neither you nor Terry will change my mind."

"I'm not going! I'm not going back to that room!"

"That's okay, you can have your mom's room. You can decorate it any way you like. How's that?"

"No! No! Please don't do this! Please!" she wailed.

"Don't argue with me. This is final. I'm not changing my mind."

~~~~~~

For the second year in a row, Jack visited Fausta's grave on August twentieth, their anniversary. He bought her a dozen red roses and placed them among the Hibiscuses that were growing like gangbusters, hiding the roses very well. He waited until it was dark and made sure nobody was around. He knelt, prayed, cried, and cursed Carly for bringing her to the US behind his back. "She needs to pay for taking my wife away from me. Why should she live and be happy?" he looked at the moonlit sky. "I promise you Faussy, she's going to pay. Dearly." Once his ritual was complete, he would cover the grave with more palm fronds, ensuring the site wouldn't attract curious eyes.

Chapter 9

Ten Years Later – Melbourne Florida

"What class do you have today?" Carly asked.

"Calculus 301."

"I'm so proud of you, you know that?" she was heaping the praise onto her adopted daughter.

"Yes, Auntie Carly, I know." She rolled her eyes, like she always did. She'd heard this over and over for the past three years.

"I know, I know, I keep saying it again and again, but I just can't get over how you've followed my career path. Just think, Nora, next year you'll be graduating, and you'll be an engineer, just like me. Oh, I'm so thrilled!" she was giddy.

"Well, I couldn't have done it without your support and patience, you know."

"I know that, too." She frowned a bit when remembering Fausta. "I just wish she was here to see you."

"You've never given up hope, have you?"

She gently grabbed Nora's hands, "I can't give up hope, Nora. Hope is all I have."

"Well, I don't think she's alive. I just can't believe that she wouldn't have made her way home somehow." She glanced at the portrait Carly had a local artist paint a few years ago, proudly displayed in the hallway.

"I know, Nora, but you've seen all those women who were kidnapped and held captive for years and years. Who knows, maybe one day somebody might hear something and report it." She tightened her lips. "I can't resign myself to her being dead. No way!"

"Whatever you want, Auntie Carly. There may be a chance, but I seriously doubt it."

"Okay, well, I'm off to work." She picked up her leather Coach bag and her car fob and headed for the door. "See you at dinner?"

"Nope. I'm going out."

Carly stopped in her tracks. "Out? And with whom, may I ask?"

"SJ." She said smiling proudly.

"Huh, SJ eh? Well, from the look on your face, he seems really nice."

"Oh, he is." Her smile widened.

Carly opened the front door. "Well, all right. Text me a photo. I'll see you later on, honeybun."

Nora crossed her arms and watched Carly from the living room window. After the attempted suicide and break up with Terrance, Carly found courage and strength to take the bull by the horns. She went to therapy, she ate right, she took yoga classes, and went back to work. Nora did her part trying not to cause Carly any stress. She went to school, got good grades, and took engineering in college. She even chose not to leave Melbourne, so she could keep an eye on Carly— who by now, was officially her mother. As a Sweet Sixteen present, Carly offered to adopt Nora and she gladly accepted. The only request she had was to keep her mom's surname and hyphen it with McIntyre. Since Nora had no relatives in the US, the adoption was easily drawn out and legalized in days.

She returned to the kitchen to make herself some breakfast. She texted SJ.

Morning.

Hey beautiful.

Can't wait till tonight.

Neither can I. □

Nora smiled as she took a bite of her waffle. They had met on campus. SJ was in the police academy, and she was taking Engineering at the Eastern Florida State College, Melbourne Campus.

SJ Daniels was almost six feet tall with chestnut hair and deep dark brown eyes. He was rather slim with broad shoulders and a tight behind. She didn't know what attracted her to him; maybe something in his eyes or his smile. Fact is that she liked him. A lot!

At the other end of the text message, SJ's smile stretched from ear to ear. Nora was gorgeous, and he still couldn't believe that she'd said yes to his invite. He'd seen her around campus, and he couldn't resist a woman who looked a lot like his favorite Italian actress, Sofia Loren. She had those same cherry blossom lips, high cheekbones, large dark eyes, long wavy auburn hair, and a bosom to die for. He noticed that she never wore tight clothing that would show off her figure. But he knew well that, with no clothes on, she was a goddess—even though he had never had the pleasure of seeing her that way. His favorite thing about her was that she did not have a tattoo. She was afraid of needles, so she claimed. That was fine with him. He didn't like tattoos either, and wasn't impressed by the new ink trend that almost every girl he ran across had signed on to. Even the police academy frowned upon tattoos, so SJ never got one. He did not want to wear a long-sleeved shirt covering his tattoos in the middle of a hot Florida summer. That would be insane!

~~~~~~

Jack was excited. He had received his concealed carry permit in the mail and now he was headed for Bass Pro Shop to buy his first gun. He'd been searching the net during the few months he had to wait for his permit, and he'd finally decided upon a Beretta M9, which was the U. S. military issued sidearm. As he drove down Babcock Street, he was in the best mood he had been in, in a long time. A tune by The Who was playing. He even had a steady girlfriend, Adaora Waweru. She was a tall, slim African woman from Kenya. Her ancestors were of blue blood, which clearly showed on her princess-like facial features. She was rather new to the US, sent there by her family to get an American education. She took Physics at F.I.T. and worked part-time at Napoli Pizza up on US Highway 1 near Sarno Road. Jack's favorite thing about her was the way he could bury his face in her huge, welcoming bosom. The fact that she worked at his favorite pizzeria was just icing on the cake, as they say. He loved going there for three reasons: one, he loved Italian food; two, he could keep a close eye on her, since he'd never lost his jealous streak; and the third and best reason, the sex was amazing. Jack thanked his lucky stars that he had a sculpted body, thanks to his daily workouts. At fifty, he was in the best shape of his life. He didn't look a day over forty. Adaora, at twenty-four, was insatiable in bed, and for the last six months, she kept him satisfied and an exceptionally happy camper.

~~~~~~

"Wow, look at you…you're a vision."

"Oh, stop, SJ." Her cheeks turned a flaming red.

"Well, it's true. That dress looks amazing on you."

Nora went all out for their date. She got her nails done, got an updo, and bought a royal blue geisha-sleeved dress with ruffles that started at the shoulder and ended at a slit just above her right knee. To top everything off, she had bought black patent stilettos which brought her eye to eye with SJ.

He kissed her lightly on the lips and pulled her chair out for her. He, too, wanted to make this date perfect. He'd made a reservation at the Gaucho Caliente, wore his favorite pinstripe suit, and rented a BMW for the occasion. He just couldn't have her get into his old jalopy. He liked Nora—a lot—and wanted to make a good impression on her.

Nora looked around. "Wow, this is nice."

"I knew you'd like it."

"Is that a salad bar?" Nora stretched to look over SJ's shoulder. Salad was her favorite.

"Yes, but the main delicacies are the different types of meat." He pointed his chin to the three waiters that were carrying large kabobs filled with several types of meat. His mouth watered at the thought.

"Oh, I love meat, too." The meat smelled awfully good. "I'm famished."

"Oh, thank God! I was afraid that you were a vegetarian."

Nora giggled. "Oh no, I love all kinds of cuisine, but I really loved my mom's dishes." Her demeanor changed to one of sadness when she said that.

"What's the matter?" SJ had immediately picked up on the change in Nora's mood.

Nora wasn't sure she wanted SJ to know about her mother. "Oh, it's nothing really. She passed away years ago."

"Oh, I'm sorry to hear that."

"It's okay. It was a long time ago."

"When did she die?"

"Ten years ago."

"Oh, I see." He took her hand and kissed it. "Do you want to talk about it?"

"It's a sad story and I don't want to ruin dinner."

One of the waiters approached and asked if they wanted any of the meat that he was carrying on the oversized skewer.

"Speaking of which…" he dug into his meat but when he noticed that Nora didn't move, he stopped. "Nora, I really want to get to know you." He picked up her left hand. "I like you a lot and I don't want to be just a boyfriend…I want to be your friend, your confidant. I want you to feel comfortable enough to tell me everything."

131

Nora stared at him for a few seconds and picked up her fork. "I appreciate that, I do, and I will tell you her story. But not right now, okay?"

"Deal." He let go her hand so she could eat. "But you will tell me, won't you?"

"I promise, I will." She dug into the small sausage and took a huge bite.

~~~~~~

Sid and Janice Daniels moved to Florida when SJ decided he didn't want to move back home. Janice missed him so much that she convinced Sid to sell their home in Mississippi and buy one in the Sunshine State. It didn't take much coaxing. After Sid had resolved the murder case of Father Nicholas, pastor of St. Gabriel Parish, he was ready to leave also. He did not want to stay in a place where he was constantly reminded of the loss of his best friend, the finest priest he had ever met. SJ was the baby of the family, so when he went off to college Janice began to search for homes. Of course, Sid acquiesced. Within a few months of Lucy's death, Sid and Janice Daniels settled in their new typical Florida home in Eau Gallie, which had been a separate city until it merged with Melbourne in 1969.

Just like every other Sunday, SJ came over to his parents for a traditional Italian dinner.

"SJ, tell me, what's new?" Janice asked as she dished out the penne.

"I met someone." He shoved some food into his mouth, not looking up, hoping that his parents hadn't heard him.

"You did? You mean, a real girl?" Janice set the pan down for Sid to serve himself. This was much more important than dinner. Sid rolled his eyes and dished out his portion.

"Yes, Mom. Her name is Nora." SJ shoveled another forkful of his mother's pasta into his mouth.

"Oh, what a pretty name." on the inside, Janice wanted to jump up and down. But she had to keep her cool. She sat down next to SJ. "Tell us about her."

"I met her at school. She's studying Engineering. She's a real Italian beauty, mom. She looks like Sofia Loren."

"Really?" that comment got Sid very interested since he secretly loved "La Loren" as she had been called during the most popular period of her life. "Go on, Son."

"Do you have a picture?"

"Actually, Mom, yes I do." He pulled out his phone and searched for a decent picture he could show. He turned the phone towards his mother. "Here she is."

Janice pulled the phone closer and put her readers on. "Wow." Was all she said. "Take a look, Sid."

SJ moved the phone so his dad could see. "Ah, yes. I must agree, she is a beauty."

"I agree." SJ placed his phone back in his pocket.

"How did you get her to go out with you?" Sid asked.

"Sid!" Janice glared at him over the top of her glasses. "Don't be rude!"

"No, it's okay, Mom. I've wondered the same thing, myself. Honestly, I don't know. We sort of bumped into each other and then I saw her here and there. Then one day, I asked her out and she said yes."

Janice saw the look in her son's eyes and her mother's instinct told her that this young woman was the one for her son. However, she kept her feelings to herself. The youths of today were so easily offended, she didn't want to rock the boat. She limited her comments the best that she could. "Well, good for you, Son."

Sid gave his wife a puzzled look as if to say, "is that all you got?" but when she shrugged her shoulders, he followed her lead. "So, when are you seeing her again?"

"After dinner."

"Well, all right then, you'd better polish off your plate. You don't want to be late, now, do you son?" Janice smiled with that Italian mother's knowing look.

"Nope!" He scarfed his food down with a twinkle in his eyes.

~~~~~~

Jack had been watching Carly for ten years now, but he could never find the right time to get even with her. *I wonder who the father of that girl is?* He asked himself. He knew she had a boyfriend of some sort, but that girl didn't look like the cop she had been dating for years. She seemed to be in her early twenties, or so, which was about how long it had been since Carly left Australia with Fausta. *Maybe some Aussie bloke knocked her up so she took off and took Fausta with her.* "Bitch!" he whispered as he pulled up his weights at the F.I.T. gym he'd been going to work out for years now. He looked at his sweaty chest that showcased the six-pack that made all the young male students envy him and the young females fawn over him like he was prince charming. He had been making plans to make her pay, but none had panned out. It had been years now, and they were still searching for Fausta. There were posters at random street intersections in Brevard County and a "Tips" hotline that rarely rang anymore. "Why don't they give up? They're never gonna find 'er." He smiled coyly as he continued lifting his weights.

~~~~~~

"You're still a virgin?" he asked as he brushed her lips gently with his.

"Yes."

He stopped for a moment to look her in the eyes. "Are you sure about this?"

Nora smiled. "Yes. I want you to be the one." She lifted her dress over her shoulders and threw it in a corner with abandon.

Very slowly, SJ resumed kissing her passionately, and slowly bringing his lips down to her neck and onto her breasts. A loud crack of thunder echoed outside, and Nora shuddered. His hands slid down her body and his entire form was moving out of her sight. He took her in his arms and placed her on his bed. He quickly shed his clothes and suddenly his chest was hovering above her hips and disappeared into the oblivion of her inviting and open legs. She saw only the top of his head and the curve of his shoulders. The unsteady rise and fall of his back coincided with his breathing. He ran his hands down and around her bare thighs, and then up again, past her ribs, around her lower back and down again, just past her hip bone. His lips touched her bare abdomen. It was just a whisper, but she melted like butter. He slid her panties down, ever so gently, and then looked at her, again.

"Are you sure?"

"Yes, please, don't stop," she begged softly, while digging her nails into his chest.

He nodded. Gently, so as not to frighten her, he entered her.

"Uh—!" Now, seeing his face, she grabbed the sheets and clenched them tightly.

"Are you okay?" He slowed his rhythm.

"Yes…" she smiled, self-consciously.

He arched his head back, while pulsing his love for her. "I love you, Nora!" he cried, as he picked up the pace.

She arched now, grinding her hips, taking in every pump. "I…I…OHHHH!" With her spasms of delight, she finished, "…love you too!"

He was waiting for this moment. A moment later, he reached his own climax, and they fell into each other's arms, trying desperately to catch their breath.

Chapter 10

Terrance was certain that this time she would accept his proposal. As he saw it, their marriage was way past due, and now that they were in a good place with Nora attending college and Carly out of that horrible mental state she had been in, he would propose again. He kept the ring the whole time, and he prayed that he would be able to finally marry the love of his life.

The only downfall was that Fausta was still missing, and even though nearly everyone had given up hope Carly never wavered. She kept telling herself that Fausta was being held captive, and on those rare occasions when police would find women who had been held prisoner for years, her hopes would brighten again. She obsessed about searching these newscasts of women being liberated and would promptly text the links to Terrance. He, in turn, would check to see if Fausta was in the list. After dozens of these stories, Terrance and Detective Sabbath had given up hope. He did not give up hope for their nuptials. It didn't matter how long it would take; he was going to convince her to marry him!

Carly knew something was up but couldn't quite put her finger on it. Terrance had invited her for a picnic on the beach, and that was not his M.O. She had a suspicion, but she held it in her heart.

Everything was perfect: the lunch bought from the deli on Hibiscus Boulevard, to the wine bought at ABC Spirits, to the sky without a cloud in sight, to the waves breaking on the sand, and the entertaining sandpipers—very small birds that somehow were able to outrun the incoming waves, not getting a drop of water on them as they plunged their beaks into the sand, looking for sand crabs and other goodies the ocean offered.

"I'm so glad I moved here, back then."

"Me too...you're the prettiest Aussie I've ever met." He pulled the ring box out the front pocket of his shorts.

"Um...you're nice but I'm not pretty anymore. Life has taken a toll on me." As much as she might want to, she couldn't frown on a day like today.

"Yes, you are." He knelt in front of her, opened the little red velvet box, and lifted the ring to her face. "You're the most beautiful woman I've ever met, you know, and I can't live without you Carly, so would you please marry me?"

Tears welled up in her eyes, and Carly did her best to stifle them. It was to no avail. "Oh, that was so clever of you."

"Good. So, say yes." He still had that smile that, try as she might, she absolutely could not resist.

Carly looked at the ring. She had forgotten how beautiful it was, and now the Florida sunshine made it gleam and twinkle like a star in the darkest of nights. She couldn't resist any longer. "Yes! Yes! I will marry you."

He removed the ring from the box. "Oh, God, finally!" he placed it on her finger. "I've waited so long for this! I love you, Carly McIntyre! I've loved you from the first time I saw your beautiful eyes." He kissed her hand and then kissed her lips like he hadn't in years. "I'm going to make you the happiest bride ever. I promise!"

"I already am." She got on her knees and kissed her fiancé passionately. "Oh, I've missed this, and I've missed you so much. I'm so sorry for what I put you through."

"All forgotten." He sat down next to her now, raising her hand to kiss it again. "Let's think about our future now."

~~~~~~

"Oh, Auntie Carly, I'm so happy for you, truly I am! You deserve happiness, and Uncle Terry is the perfect man for you!"

"Yes." She could not stop looking at her ring. "The time has come to think about the future." She smiled at Nora. "You're sure you're good with all this?"

"Absolutely. You suffered enough. You deserve to have some of your own happiness. We both do." She hugged her auntie tightly.

Carly took both of Nora's hands in her own and gently squeezed them. "Yes, you're right, we both do." She hugged her niece tighter.

"All right, then, now that it's settled, when's the wedding?"

"Oh, we haven't set a date yet. But it will be on the beach, for sure."

"Oh, that sounds exciting! I love beach weddings."

"Me too." She picked up her key fob. "We'll talk later on, okay? Gotta get to work." She opened the front door.

"Okay, love you!"

"Love you, too, Honeybun." She closed the door behind her.

As Carly drove off, Jack attentively watched her car leak precious brake fluid with every touch of the pedal. With an evil grin, he started his pickup and followed behind her—without getting too close, of course. He had never done this before, and his sick, twisted mind wanted to see how it played out. "Gotta make sure you pay what you owe me." With the liquid still leaking, her car reached the top of the railroad overpass on R. J. Conlan Boulevard. She pressed the brake pedal to slow for her turn onto Dixie Highway. The pedal sank all the way to the floor. She panicked. She pressed the brake pedal even harder. Still, nothing. It again sank all the way to the floor. One more time. Pushing hard on the brake pedal, it went all the way to the floor.

In her panicked state, she failed to navigate the turn onto Dixie Highway. She hit the curb full on, at 50 miles per hour. The car continued onward, right between two cabbage palm trees, and sailed over the forty-foot-high bluff along the bank of the Indian River Lagoon. The water was not deep enough for the car to sink—only two or three feet. But as the car went down, it landed head-on, and then rolled onto its roof. The crash killed her instantly. Blunt force trauma, the Medical Examiner's report would label it. In the blink of an eye, Jack had gotten the revenge he had been seeking for over ten years.

"See ya in hell!" he yelled as he drove by the scene, knowing full well that she could not hear him.

~~~~~~

"Oh my God! Auntie Carly! Nooooo!" Nora fell to her knees. "Not her too! No! No!"

Terrance pulled her into his arms, thinking back on the last time this young girl lost someone she loved. "I'm so sorry, Nora. So, so sorry."

"Again! Again! Why me? Why me?" She held tightly onto Terrance as she sobbed uncontrollably. "Why, Uncle Terry? Why her? You were supposed to be married! No! No!"

"It was a terrible accident." His thoughts belied his words.

"But why? Why her? Why, God, why? Why take her? Hadn't she suffered enough? Haven't I suffered enough? I hate You! I hate You! I hate You!" she cried into Terrance's strong chest.

He held her as tightly as he could without hurting her, not letting her go. He nodded while he squeezed his own eyes shut, letting the tears flow. He could not disagree with her. *Why is God so cruel? What the hell did Carly ever do to deserve this?* He had begged her not to buy that car, but she didn't listen. And now some manufacturer's defect took another life. It took the life of his beloved, and someone was going to pay.

They were out on F.I.T.'s front lawn. SJ came running after Terrance had texted him. He pulled Nora into his strong arms and held her as tightly as he could. She was convulsing as she wept. His heart broke for his girlfriend who now had nobody. "I'm here. I'm here. I'm not going anywhere."

A small crowd was gathering and in the midst of that crowd, Jack was watching closely. He felt for her. *Must have been tough to lose your mother like that. And so suddenly.* He pursed his lips and shook his head in genuine empathy for the young lady. "Unfortunate, indeed," he mumbled, and went back to his job.

"Come, let me take you home."

"No! I don't want to go home. I can't go back to that house again. Not after all this. I just can't!"

SJ looked up at Terrance. "That's fine, we'll go to my place." He gently led her toward his lifted F-150. He opened the passenger door and helped her in. He quickly got in and drove very slowly to his apartment building in Suntree, a drive of about 25 miles.

During the trip, Nora didn't take her eyes off the Indian River Lagoon. She was beginning to loathe this place. It had taken her mom and now her adopted mom. "I'm leaving."

"What? Why?" That had come out of the blue.

"Because this stupid town has taken my mom and my adoptive mom! I hate it here, now!"

SJ began to panic inwardly as he kept his eyes on the road. She wanted to leave, and he understood why, but he couldn't lose her. Not now. Not ever.

They arrived at his apartment.

"You take my room. I'll sleep on the couch."

"I can't do that. This is your place."

"You're taking my bed, and that's all there is to it! Now, hush!"

She heard the determination in his voice. His authoritative voice actually soothed her. Right now, she needed someone to take control.

When he finally got her tucked in, he dried her tears with his fingers. "Nora, I know you're upset, and you have every right to be. But please, don't leave now. Please."

"No, I'm leaving tomorrow. I don't care, anymore."

"Okay, okay." He had to think quickly. "Let's make a pact."

"What pact?"

"Let's finish school first, and then we can go wherever you want. Deal?"

She nodded, exhausted, and faded into slumber.

After closing his bedroom door, SJ texted Terrance in a panic.

She wants to leave.

Leave? Where?

I don't know. She's tired of this place. She lost two parents, she said.

Two parents?

Yeah, long story.

I got all night. Call me.

Terrance called SJ and told him the entire story as he knew it.

"Oh my God, I had no clue."

146

"I thought you two were intimate."

"We are, but she never told me that her mom was murdered. She only told me that she died. So, I assumed it had been a car accident or some deathly disease, of some sort." Holding the phone to his ear, SJ tiptoed into his bedroom to make sure Nora was still sleeping.

"Yeah, it took Carly years to get over Fausta's death. To this day, she hoped that Fausta would show up one day, out of the…blue." His voice cracked.

"Fausta was her mom's name?"

"Yes."

"You know, she didn't even tell me that."

"Wow, she must have buried that pain very deep."

"I guess."

"So, make sure to bring Nora to Dr. Osbourne. He really did a great job with Carly. It took several years, but his professional help really brought Carly back to normalcy."

"Oh?"

"Yes. And believe me, it was tough. Really tough."

"Okay, man, will do. I'll talk to her in the morning."

"Yeah, I'll send you his info. But SJ. Give her a few days to mourn. Okay?"

"Oh, for sure," SJ replied, while wondering how he was going to do that.

"Just be by her side and pamper her. Then in a few days, you guys can talk about Dr. Osbourne." It was almost as if Terrance was reading his thoughts.

"Okay, will do. Thanks for the advice."

"It's my pleasure."

SJ ended the call and checked on Nora one more time before he tried to catch a few winks on his not-so-comfy couch.

~~~~~~

When Nora entered Dr. Osbourne's office, it brought her mind right back to the times she'd waited for Carly to finish her sessions. After Fausta's disappearance, Carly would not let Nora out of her sight, bringing her almost everywhere with her. Nora sat on the very chair as she had back then. Somehow, the office seemed much smaller, now. The many Space Shuttle photos were all still there—except, after all these years, many more were added. Nora rose and walked up to those pictures to have a closer look. As her eyes passed from one photo to the other, she recalled watching some of those launches with her classmates, and some with Auntie Carly and her mom. Her vision became obscured by a watery glaze.

"Miss Benito, Dr. Osbourne will see you now," the receptionist announced.

The huge white door wasn't so white or so huge, anymore.

"Come in, Miss Benito. Have a seat."

As she entered his office, she noticed even more photos of the shuttle. The left wall really stood out. It was covered with photos, newspaper clippings, and other souvenirs of the Shuttle Challenger that suffered a catastrophic end to its flight on January 28, 1986. Right in the center of it all, was the epic photo of the fireball and the grotesquely twisted vapor trails of the solid rocket boosters in uncontrolled flight. It was a defining moment in the American Space Program, and profoundly affected every resident on the Space Coast of Florida.

"Very sad, isn't it?" Dr. Osbourne's voice quivered, even after all these years. "You see that young astronaut there?" He pointed toward Ronald McNair's photo.

"Yes."

"He went to school with my son." Dr. Osbourne had a knot in his throat. "He was a good boy, he was. And smart. He had to be smart to make it on the Challenger crew."

Nora looked at those people with profound sympathy and respect. Her aunt always had good things to say about the NASA astronauts, many of them Eagle Scouts.

"Indeed, he was. But why do you keep these memorabilia on display? Doesn't it make you sad? Aren't you dwelling on the negative?"

"Yes, it is sobering. But it reminds me of the fragility of life, and the fact that tomorrow is not guaranteed to me, you, or anyone else. Even this afternoon isn't guaranteed."

Therein began Nora's therapy. Three years later, she graduated from University of Central Florida at the top of her class, with a Bachelor of Science degree in Aerospace Engineering. She was looking at excellent job opportunities with two major NASA subcontractors. SJ had already graduated from the police academy and was next in line for promotion to sergeant. He never left her side, watching her slowly heal, with a great admiration and reverence for the woman that he could no longer live without.

Jack was still working in the same position at F.I.T. He was content with the money he was making and made sure not to rock the boat. He had gotten what he wanted, and he really enjoyed living in Florida. He also kept himself quite fit so the young college ladies would swoon over him. That kept his ego pumped. His girlfriend Adaora had now become his fiancée, but he was not anywhere near ready to commit to marriage. He would not make that same mistake twice. Besides, he was happy with the way things were. Why fix what's not broken? Adaora climbed the ladder to success, becoming head hostess for the incredibly popular, upscale Italian restaurant on the Space Coast, "Passione di Pasta," where the tastiest and most original pasta dishes were served. When it opened in 2019, it became extremely popular right away. Reservations had to be made months in advance. As Adaora's income increased, so did her desire to settle down. She bought a two-bedroom condominium on U.S. 1, facing the Indian River Lagoon. The view of the lagoon seemed to change daily, making her heart skip a beat.

Chapter 11

"Marry me."

"What?" she could not believe what she just heard.

"I know, it's out of the blue but I love you and I've loved you since that first day I saw you on campus. Please say yes!"

They were enjoying a lazy Sunday morning, lounging in bed.

"Where's this coming from?" she was thrilled at what she heard but wanted to push back. Just a little.

SJ turned on his side and faced her. "I really don't know. I love you. That's all. And I want to spend the rest of my life with you." The he smacked himself on his forehead. "Damn, I don't even have a ring." He shot out of bed. "Come on, let's go ring shopping. I want you to have the perfect ring."

"No."

SJ frowned, hunched over, he sat back on his bed with his back to her. "No? But why?" he bowed his head and closed his eyes.

Nora got on her knees and crawled behind SJ wrapping her arms around him. "I mean yes, I'll marry you but no, I don't want to go ring shopping."

SJ got down on his knees with a huge smile from ear to ear. "Really, you'll marry me?"

Nora nodded.

He gave her a puzzled look. "Then why don't you want a ring?"

Nora hopped off the bed and quickly went into the closet. She uncovered one of the plastic totes and hurriedly searched for a small red velvet box. She ran back to the bed, sat on it as she opened the little box. "Because, I already have a ring." She moved the shiny diamond ring closer to his view.

"What? Who? How?"

Nora laughed whole heartedly. "It was Auntie Carly's engagement ring. Uncle Terry thought I should keep it since he had no use for it."

SJ pulled it out of the box and examined it. "It's beautiful, for sure."

"Yes, and it was given to Carly with a world of love. So, no need to spend money when I already have a symbol of love. We can turn it into a symbol of our love. What do you say?" she cocked her head hoping for a positive reaction.

"Yes! I love the idea." He slid it on her finger. "I love you Nora and I can't wait to be your husband."

"I love you too." She kissed her husband-to-be passionately as she pulled him back into bed.

~~~~~~

I got the job!

> *You did?*

Yes! I'm so excited!

> *I'll bet you are! When do you start?*

Next Monday.

> *Well, we need to celebrate. Now, we have two things to celebrate.*

Yes, we do. ☐

> *What do you think about "Passione di Pasta"?*

Oh, wow! That's the hottest and most expensive place in town.

> *I don't care. You deserve it!*

You know there's a waiting list, right SJ?

> *I know…but I got connections…☐*

Oh, okay. I want to see if you can pull this off.

> *Oh, I will. ☐*

"Wow, look at this place! It's gorgeous!" The elegantly dressed maître d' pulled the chair out for Nora. After she was seated, she set her left hand flat on the table to show off her ring. She moved her hand slightly, causing the

155

diamond to sparkle and glimmer. "I love you." She was ecstatic, and the excitement was bursting forth. SJ seated himself across from Nora. He just couldn't keep his eyes off her.

Another waiter, dressed in a perfectly cleaned and pressed tuxedo, brought their menus. "I shall return in a jiffy." He bowed and left.

Their table was not too far from the front desk where they had been greeted by a stunning black woman wearing a sleek black evening gown that had a slit all the way up to her hip.

Nora was mesmerized by her beauty and elegance. "I swear, she must be wearing a Dolce e Gabana original." Then she noticed an older man approach her and sensually wrap his arm around her waist. She melted, slightly, into his embrace. From where she was seated, she couldn't make out his face. Nora smiled, though, as she noticed the black woman turn to give the man a sensual kiss. She surmised that the black woman was seemed to be in the same moment as she: filled with love for her man.

"G'day darlin'. Well blow me down! Finally found ya, slag!"

The black woman giggled and hooked her arm into his. They exited the restaurant with their backs to Nora and SJ.

Nora's flute of champagne went crashing down onto the marble floor, shattering into pieces. She felt like she had just been punched in the gut. Suddenly, she was transported back, over a decade, into that closet, peeking out of the doors, trying to make out who was taking her mom. She sat frozen, the color quickly evaporating from her face. Still looking at the restaurant entrance, she kept a stone face, mesmerized, not moving a muscle. She couldn't even blink.

"Nora? Nora?" SJ asked as he waved his hand in front of her face. Still no movement. He was starting to get concerned. He got up and stood directly in front of her. "Nora, babe, are you okay?" he snapped his fingers.

Nora suddenly got a fearful look on her face. It was as though she had seen a ghost. "Huh?"

"What happened Nora? What did you see?"

She stood up and let the napkin fall to her feet. "Take me home." She quickly walked away.

SJ blinked in shock. "But we haven't..." then he noticed her evening purse that she left behind. He quickly picked it up and ran after her. He tried stopping her. "Nora, slow down. Please. What's going on?"

"I want to go home! Now!" She walked out stomping her heels. All the while, she was white as a ghost and shaking like a leaf.

"Okay, okay, let's go." SJ was terrified. He looked back into the restaurant to see what could have caused her to become so upset. In the blink of an eye, she was transformed from a confident, loving fiancée into a fragile, terrified little girl who wanted to run and hide.

"Where's the damn car?" she paced up and down, not anywhere near having calmed down at all.

"He'll be here." He touched her arm to try and stop her.

"Don't touch me!" She abruptly pulled her arm away from SJ and placed herself at least ten feet away.

After what seemed an eternity, the valet arrived with SJ's perfectly detailed Jeep.

"Finally!" she quickly got into the passenger side and buckled up.

SJ thanked and tipped the valet, hopped in, and sped away. He didn't want to share his embarrassment with anyone else. He stayed quiet for several minutes; then he mustered up some courage. "Nora, please talk to me. I'm here for you. please?"

Nora's crossed arms slowly morphed to both hands covering her eyes as she shook with silent, agonizing sobs.

God, he wished he knew what to say. "Can we go see my parents? My mom makes some terrific tea, and my dad is a fantastic listener." He had to do something and going to his parents was all he could think about.

As her sobbing became more pronounced, she nodded.

He thanked his lucky stars that his parents' house was not far away. He knew his parents would know what to do, especially his father who had been in law enforcement for so long that he'd become an expert in reading people.

Ten minutes later, SJ was helping Nora out of the Jeep. He guided her to his parents' front door and rang the doorbell.

"SJ? Nora? Wha…" his mother looked surprised.

SJ placed his finger to his lips, as he gently guided Nora to the living room where he sat her on the couch. "Mom, we need your tea, now." He cocked his head toward the kitchen. As they entered the kitchen, he whispered; "Mom, please, just make that famous calming tea and bring it to her. Please? I'm getting Dad."

Janice nodded without saying a word and started pulling out the Bonomelli Chamomilla tea she had bought in an Italian bakery. Her mother had made it all the time when anyone in the family was ill or upset. She swore it could solve any situation and she prayed that it would do its magic again now.

SJ burst into his dad's ham radio room. Sid had his radio headset on, with a boom microphone in front of his mouth.

"Dad, I need you!" SJ interrupted his father's ham radio conversation.

When Sid looked at the frightened look on his son's face, he immediately knew something was terribly wrong. "Hey, guys, something's going on here that I need to handle. 73, all. AI4GK is clear.

"What is it, son?"

"It's Nora, dad, I…" his voice cracked.

"What? Did you get into an accident?"

"No, no, we didn't."

"What is it then?" he was becoming anxious.

"I took Nora out to dinner at Passione di Pasta to celebrate our engagement."

"Oh, excellent choice. But go on."

SJ took a deep breath. "We had just sat at our table, and everything was fine, great…"

"Go on."

"Then something happened, but I don't know what exactly. Out of nowhere, Nora became angry and upset. She just got up and stormed out. She ordered me to take her home. I've never seen her like this, not even when her auntie died…"

"Yes, how tragic."

"Then when we got in the Jeep, she broke down, so I thought to bring her here. I hope that's okay."

"Of course, Son." He looked towards the kitchen.

"I asked mom to make her famous tea, but I need you to talk to her and find out what set her off."

"Sure Son." Sid got up from his chair, turned off the ham radio, and followed his son into the living room. Just as they arrived and made themselves comfortable, Janice arrived with the tea. Sid could not help but notice the makeup streaming down Nora's face and how she trembled. He got the throw and placed it gently around her shoulders. "Better?"

Again, just a silent nod.

"Here, Nora, have some of this tea. It's a godsend." She handed the cup to her. "Sugar?"

As Nora took the cup in her quivering hands, it rattled on the saucer and a few drops spilled out. She shook her head and took a sip of the tea. In short order, the warm liquid began to calm her, and warmed her up inside. "Mmmmm." She whispered.

"Told ya," SJ said.

"You were right. This tea is amazing, Mrs. Daniels."

"Oh, please! Mrs. Daniels was my mother-in-law. Janice works just fine."

161

Nora cracked a smile as she softly blew on her tea to help cool it.

Janice cocked her head toward the men to get them to leave the room. Like two rockets, they bolted from the living room. Janice sat next to Nora, placed her hand on the young woman's arm, and patted it gently. "So, do you want to talk about it?"

"Oh Janice, I can't even..." She said through her sobs. "It's a very long story."

Janice pulled a tissue from the box and handed it to Nora. "I've got nothing but time."

Nora dried her eyes and began telling the story of Fausta, starting at that fatal afternoon. The words flowed nonstop from her lips. Janice was horrified at what she was being told. She kept her cool, though, as she looked at SJ and Sid quietly standing in the kitchen, just outside the living room, listening with rapt attention to every word that came from Nora.

"It was the exact same voice saying the exact same phrase, and the memory of that day literally knocked the breath out of me! That's why I got so upset. I just can't forget that man's voice."

Janice saw a drop of moisture glisten in the young woman's eyes, mixed with terror and sadness. Instinctively, she hugged Nora and held her as tightly as she could. "I'm so sorry, I'm so sorry." She rocked her gently as she kept her hold. "Let it out, sweetie, let it out. You're safe here."

Chapter 12

Jack was so excited. He couldn't wait to tell Adaora that he wanted to get married and take her to Australia for their honeymoon. At this point in his life, he felt secure enough to start a new life, which included a new wife, and perhaps a few kids too. All dressed up in a dark gray pinstripe suit, a pearl-white shirt that matched his teeth, and a bright yellow sixties-style necktie with pink flamingos, he breezed into the "Passione di Pasta" Restaurant. Removing his Armani sunglasses, he slid them into his front jacket pocket. His ravenous ego was being nourished by the approving glances of the young ladies. "There she is," he whispered, when he saw his precious Adaora facing the dining room. Every time she gestured with her left hand; he noticed the sparkling new diamond ring glittering in the LED lighting. He stealthily crept up on her from behind and hugged her. "Gidday darlin'. Well blow me down! Finally found ya, slag!"

A sudden shattering of glass rang out, but Adaora was interested only in the man with his arms around her waist. She turned around to give him a provocative kiss.

"Are you ready, Darlin'?" As Jack gently kissed the back of her neck, he detected a slight shiver from his lady.

"Can't wait for what's in store."

"Come on, then." He took her hand, kissed it, and gently led her toward the entrance. This time the looks were on for Adaora from many men with desire in their hearts for this beautiful black woman. Jack was not jealous; on the contrary, he was proud that his future wife was one of the most beautiful women he had ever met. Just for a fleeting moment, he mentally compared her to Fausta., he shook that thought immediately. She's long gone, and his future was with Adaora now.

As they approached his truck, she stopped him. "Oh, I almost forgot my purse. Let me go in the back door. I'll be right back."

"Sure, Love." He put his sunglasses back on, folded his muscular arms, and leaned against the old but cleaned pickup truck. He rested his left foot on the right front tire. The young couple exiting the restaurant caught his attention. The man was holding onto the young lady, in an apparent attempt to hold her up. *Is she limping? Doesn't look like it. She sure seems upset, though.* As they made their way to SJ's shiny Jeep, Jack glared at her. *I know her.* But he couldn't quite put his finger on it. The young man helped her into his Jeep and quickly went to the driver's side, got in, started the engine, and took off. Suddenly, it dawned on him. "Yeah, Carly's girl."

"Here I am." Adaora was by his side again. "Who were you talking to?"

"No-one, Love. Let's go." He helped his fiancée into his pickup, then rushed to the driver's side. "We've got a new life to live." He cranked the engine. "Are ya ready slag?"

"I am." She was ecstatic at the sudden turn of her life. Up to a week or so ago, she was in a relationship going nowhere, quickly. Then, as Jack was good at doing, he surprised her with an engagement ring and a proposal, which she accepted without hesitation. Wedding in two weeks and honeymoon in Australia. All this while knowing little about Jack's past. All she knew was that he was built, and that he had an Aussie accent. What more did she need? She looked at her sparkling, new diamond ring while her thoughts wandered to a few years in the future, where she imagined a single-story Florida home, a big dog in the fenced-in back yard, and two or three kids.

"Penny for your thoughts." Jack snapped her out of her reverie.

"Oh, nothing really. I was just thinking about our future together." She turned to face him. "I wonder; why the sudden change?"

"I just love you, that's all. I don't want to lose you." He failed to tell her that, in reality his beloved Fausta had been dead for over ten years, and it was time to begin a new life with a new wife. He had gone to visit her burial ground, which by now was overrun by the hibiscuses and the cabbage palms and prairie grass. The last time he went, he had to machete his way to her grave. He knelt and begged for her forgiveness. Somehow, he felt that he received it. It could have been from the sound of the fluttering breeze, or the chirp of Florida crow, or the screech of the hawk, or some combination of the three. In his head it was a concerto of approval for Jack to continue on with his life. *And so be it.*

Adaora wrapped her arms around Jack's stone-hard bicep and rested her head on his shoulder. "I'm so excited, Jack."

"Me too, love, me too." Jack made a right turn onto Nasa Boulevard.

"Where are we going?"

"To the bridal shop."

"Bridal shop? But...but...you..."

"Yes, Love, I know...the groom isn't suppos'ta see the bride, but I thought I'd drop you off and come pick ya up later on."

"Okay." She looked puzzled. "You're leaving me at the shop by myself?"

"No worries, Love, you have company waitin' for ya."

Hmmmm. I wonder what he's up to.

Jack laughed wholeheartedly and blasted the music which seemed to fill the streets. He got to Downtown Bridal rather quickly and stopped right in front. There was a group of women waiting, and when the vehicle approached, they started jumping, clapping, and screaming with joy.

"Oh my God, Jack, what did you do?" Her huge smile sent Jack to Seventh Heaven. Then she turned to the group of women consisting of her mother, sister, and work colleagues. They all were very close to Adaora and when she descended from the truck, they all huddled in a tight group, kissing, hugging, and talking incessantly. Excitement permeated the air.

Smiling, he whispered to himself, "I did the right thing, I did," knowing full well that no one was listening.

~~~~~~

Ever since that episode with Nora, something wasn't sitting right with Sid. He did not want to get involved, because Nora was his son's girlfriend. But on the other hand, he *wanted* to get involved—because Nora was his son's girlfriend. He felt duty-bound. The girl's mother was killed, and her body was never found. Not to mention, Nora's Aunt Carly, who also died suspiciously. Her mother's body could be anywhere from Melbourne, Australia to Melbourne

Florida. Finding her killer was going to be a huge undertaking. He would have to travel to Australia. And heck, that was a very long flight. With his bladder? That flight would be brutal. But a woman's life was taken, and he had become quite fond of that woman's daughter. *I'll do it.* Now he had to let SJ and Nora know his intentions, but he had no clue how to begin the conversation. He wondered if Janice was willing to sweeten the deal with one of her wonderful Italian meals. It was worth a try. He pulled out his cell, found his wife's number, and hit call.

"Hey, Sid."

"Hey Honey. Listen, I have to ask you something."

"Hmmm, let me guess…you want to find Nora's mother's killer."

"But how?"

"Oh, come on, Sid. How long have we been married?"

"I know, but how did you figure it out?"

"Honey. Nora is dating Junior, and I know that you've taking a liking to her, haven't you?"

"Yes."

"Well, I knew that the other night when she started talking about how her mother died and how her body was never found and how she never understood why she was killed, that spark in your eyes reappeared. It's like clockwork. Don't forget, I know you!"

Sid's heart filled with even more love for his wife of thirty-seven years. Of course, she was one hundred percent right. She knew him inside and out, and she always was one step ahead of him. He never figured out how she did it. "Do you know how amazing you are?"

Janice smiled. "Yeah, yeah, I know." Waving him off.

"I'm on my way home. Do I need to pick anything up?"

"Nope. I'll dig up your passport."

"What for?"

"Well, duh! You'll be traveling to Australia, right?"

~~~~~~

"Oh, my Lord! A forty-eight-hour flight! That's brutal!" Sid was shouting at the computer screen. "And look at that price! Holy mackerel!"

"Oh, come on, you're not going to be in an airplane the whole time. Look…" Janice pointed at the screen. "you're stopping in Atlanta first, and you'll be there for a couple of hours. Then you're stopping again in Los Angeles, and you'll be there for…let's see…" she clicked next. "Four-and-a-half hours. You see? That shaves plenty of time off the flight."

"Sure, that removes six and a half hours, but I'm spending a whopping forty-two hours in the air." He shook

171

his head. "If this doesn't kill me, nothing will. I'm too old for this crap!"

"Oh, you'll be fine." She slapped him softly on his shoulder. "It's for a good cause, you know. Besides, not going will kill you more than this flight."

"I guess," he grunted.

Then she had a thought. She sat down next to him and lowered the laptop screen. "What if I come with you?" she raised her eyebrows in query.

"Oh?"

"Yes, I could go sightseeing while you do your investigating. I'll keep you company on the flight, so it won't be so bad."

Sid looked at his wife and smiled. Without skipping a beat, she always knew what he needed. "Okay. But it's going to cost us."

She shrugged her shoulders. "So? It will be our major trip for this year. Besides, Australia is on our bucket list, right?"

"Right." He kissed her cheek. "Have I told you lately how much I love you?"

"You just did." She got up. "I'll make some espresso. It looks like we've got some work to do."

With a satisfied look on his face, Sid lifted the laptop screen back up and continued his search.

~~~~~~

"Terrance Bouchuroix, I presume?" Sid got up.

"Yes, Mr. Daniels?" Terrance had some streaks of gray hair, but his muscular body was still in ship-shape.

"Please. Call me Sid." He extended his hand to the young detective.

Terrance shook it with muscle—but not too much. "Terry is good for me."

"Good, so now that we've settled the name situation, let's get down to business, shall we?" they simultaneously sat down in the "Espresso-land" coffee shop.

"Oh, so no wasting time. I like that."

"Thanks, Detective." Sid waved to one of the young girls behind the counter.

"Oh, no, you have to go to the counter and order."

"Awww geez!" reluctantly Sid got up and headed for the counter.

"No, wait, I'll go." Terrance stopped him, since it was obvious that Sid did not want to go.

"Oh, thanks." Sid really disliked these modern-day restoration places. Whatever happened to waiters and waitresses? Now, all you get is servers.

"What do you want?" Terrance asked, pulling out his wallet.

"Just plain old coffee. Black, please. Oh, and hot. I don't go for all this iced stuff."

Terrance gave him a thumbs up. "Yeah. Me either, to be honest."

A few minutes later, both men were sitting across from each other, their hands wrapped around two mugs of hot, steaming, black coffee.

"So, tell me about Fausta Benito."

Terrance took a deep breath and told her story from the day he met her through Carly. He described how the county searched for her for over a year after she was killed, and then labeled it a cold case. He explained how Carly had taken it so badly that she had to get psychological help to overcome the burden of guilt, and that she never fully recovered. Finally, after eleven years, he convinced her to get married. And then she, too, died tragically and mysteriously.

"So was Fausta's body ever found?"

Terrance shook his head, frowning.

"What about Carly? Did you resolve her case?"

"No. We pulled her car from the river, but with all the water the car took in, we couldn't do a proper forensic investigation. So, it was deemed an accident and closed as such."

"What about Jack Renolds?"

"Never found. We don't even know what he looks like."

"No? Why?"

"He kept his back to Nora throughout the whole ordeal. All she was able to do was hear his voice."

"Wow, what tough luck." He shook his head in disbelief. "That poor girl. She must have gone to hell and back."

"She did. In fact, she, too, had a nervous breakdown when Carly died, but SJ stuck with her and so did I, and slowly but surely, she came out of it."

"Were you able to get me the case files?"

"Yeah, sure. Both cases are closed, and all files are public record so…" he pulled out two manila folders, both sealed with string, and handed them to Sid. "Here you go. Have at it."

"Thanks." He opened his computer bag and slid the folders inside. "How much do I owe you, Terry."

"Nothing. It was an honor." He stood up. "You know, your reputation precedes you."

Sid looked puzzled. "What do you mean?"

"Well, when Nora told me about you, I did a bit of digging and found out about the case you solved back in Mississippi."

"But how…"

"Now, that's a dumb question, don't you think? Mr. Google knows all!" He extended his hand.

"Yeah, you're right, there." Sid shook his hand. "I'll bring these back as soon as possible."

"No problem, man, hang on to them as long as you want. Just get this asshole!" he walked out.

Sid watched him leave as his thoughts drifted to Father Nicholas. Even after all this time, he still missed him dearly.

Chapter 13

Two weeks later Jack and Adaora were lined up at the Melbourne International Airport, passports in hand, waiting to pass security.

"Are you excited?"

She flashed a huge smile his way. "Can't you tell?" she asked, with a hint of mischief in her voice.

He gave his wife a warm hug and a slight nod. As they approached security, he placed all his gadgets, along with hers, in the plastic bin. Then he placed both carry-on bags on the rollers and watched them being transported into the x-ray machine. Jack attentively watched each and every person around him with a bit of concern. A few drops of sweat formed on his brow. But everyone was being normal, not giving him and his bride a second thought, as they all moved forward. Once they passed security and headed toward their gate, Jack was completely relaxed. He wiped the few drops of perspiration with his shirt cuff.

"Are you okay, babe?"

"Couldn't be better, Love." He took a seat and pulled out his phone to check any alerts. "I'm thirsty." He got up, "Want anything, Love?"

"No, thanks."

He went to the café to buy a bottle of water. When he returned, the crew already had begun boarding procedures.

"That was quick."

"Yep, we should be shoving off around 3." Adaora hooked her arm into her husband's.

Jack opened his passport to glance at his boarding passes. The flight from Atlanta to LAX wouldn't leave until nine fifteen, so they would have a layover of several hours. There would be another wait in Los Angeles. All this waiting made Jack uneasy. *What if someone recognizes me?* That was a chance he would have to take.

~~~~~~

"What time is our flight?"

"Six fifty-five." Janice glanced at her boarding pass.

"So, we get there around eight thirty, right?"

"Yes, and our connecting flight to Los Angeles takes off at nine fifteen."

"Wow, that's cutting it close. I won't even have time to take a leak."

"Now, Sid, we talked about this. They won't leave until everyone has boarded. You'll have plenty of time."

Janice was already regretting tagging along. Sid was such a complainer sometimes.

"All right, don't get snippy."

"Sid, Honey. I love you, but sometimes you're a real pain in the ass. You know that, right?"

Sid rolled his eyes and shrugged his shoulders. "I'm just nervous, is all."

"Hey, I know. That's why I'm here to support you and listen to your bitching— but most of all, to help you enjoy this trip."

Sid placed their carry-ons on the rollers and gently pushed them toward the x-ray machine. "I'm just not looking forward to these three long flights." he headed for the body scanning machine.

"I know...I know." she entered right after he was cleared. "But the flight to Atlanta is going to be short and sweet."

"Probably the only one." he grabbed both carry-ons and rolled them to their gate. When they arrived there, they found not many people waiting.

"Oh, nice, looks like our flight is going to be fairly empty."

"I hope so."

~~~~~

"That was an excruciating seven hours!" Sid was almost ready to turn around.

"Oh, it wasn't that bad." Janice sometimes felt like the court jester, working hard to try everything to lighten Sid's mood. There was no way she could put up with him for another sixteen hours! "Come on, I see an espresso stand. Let's get one."

Sid shook his head and followed his wife. He certainly could use an espresso right about now.

As they sat at the small table to enjoy their espresso, Janice pulled out her boarding passes and examined them. "Huh, row seventeen, seats D and E. I guess those would be the middle seats."

"I just hope they're not too far from the bathroom."

"Shouldn't be. I specifically asked the lady at the check in to give us seats that were close to the bathrooms and both flights we just took were indeed close. So, I don't see why these wouldn't be."

"I sure hope you're right." he sipped his coffee. "Geez, fifteen hours..."

"Sixteen, plus deplaning, getting our baggage, and getting to our hotel." she took the last bite of her Cannoli. Janice figured since Sid was already turning dour, she'd just rub it in as much as she could. She was really tiring of his moodiness. "And don't forget the eight-hour drive to Melbourne, but we should be fully rested by then."

"We should be." Their plans were to stay in Sydney for a few days, then rent a car and drive to Melbourne.

"Oh, says on this website..."

"What website?"

"The Traveling Boomers dot com."

"Oh okay, go on."

"It says Australians drive on the left, like in the UK."

"Oh great, another country that drives on the wrong side of the road. Geez."

"Oh, but they have grilled kangaroo."

"What? Well, I'm not having any of that."

"Oh, come on! Broaden your horizons, Sid! It says here that it's quite tasty and has lots of iron, too." she showed her screen to Sid. "We'll just try a small piece, okay? But you've got to try it."

Sid threw his hands in the air. "Fine, okay, I'll try it."

Janice got up and threw out her paper espresso cup and her napkin. "Good, cause I'm not going to have all the fun on my own, do you hear me?"

"Yes, dear." he replied in a low voice. That was his cue to comply.

~~~~~~

"Mr. And Mrs. Reynolds, row eighteen, seats D and E. Enjoy your flight." The flight attendant handed the boarding passes back to the newlyweds.

"Thank you." Adaora took both passes and began walking down the center rows of the plane, searching for her seats. "Sixteen, seventeen. Oh. Here we are. Eighteen." she opened the compartment, placed her carry-on neatly inside, and took her seat in the center, crossing her long dark legs, of course, giving a sensual smile to her husband.

"Oh, this is nice, not too far from the loo."

She cuddled up to Jack and whispered in his ear. "Do you want to join the mile high club later on?"

"I'd love ta, ya slag." he kissed her passionately. He hadn't been looking forward to this long flight, but slowly, he was beginning to change his mind.

"These seats aren't too bad, right?" Janice asked Sid, as she made herself comfortable.

"They're okay." Sid sat down in the aisle seat, right after stowing their carry-ons away in the overhead compartments. "I see it's very close to the bathroom."

"Told ya." Janice giggled.

As Sid settled in, he scrutinized every man who came and went on the flight, including the male flight attendants. He paid extra attention to the ones with Aussie accents, which seemed to him to be nearly every man who appeared to be around the age of Jack: early to mid-fifties, muscular, with dark hair. That was all he knew. He never received any information from the Aussie authorities, hence his trip. He wanted to speak with Melbourne law enforcement and try to get whatever they had on this guy. He was determined to find this killer, if it was the last thing he did.

"Jack." Sid heard that name being called out and searched to see who would respond. The younger male flight attendant turned, and Sid noticed his name tag: Jacques, but most probably he was called Jack. This man was too young to be his suspect. *One down,* Sid made a mental note.

About a few hours into the flight, Sid heard some giggling and what seemed like smooching coming from the seats behind him. He tried to turn to see who it was and saw a very beautiful black woman gazing lovingly into the eyes of the man sitting next to her.

"Oh, Jack, we're getting closer. I can't wait to meet your family."

Sid didn't think anything of it. He assumed her 'Jack' was also black. So, he made himself comfortable, put on his eyeshades, pulled his airline blanket up over his shoulders, and dozed off.

Sid looked around and noticed a bunch of men who looked the same. They were all quite tall, dark haired, muscular and they all looked like they were in their early fifties. Then he noticed a number of women who looked like Fausta, all with open arms and all calling Jack. But she was dead. How could this be?

Jack!

Jack!

Jack!

Sid abruptly awoke, and after a moment of acclimating to wakefulness, realized that he was back in reality. He blinked a few times to clear his vision, when he noticed a man coming out of the lavatory. The man was quite tall, had dark hair, was full of muscle, and looked like he was in his mid-forties. He did not have a receding hairline, and he could have dyed his hair. Sid sat up straight and looked attentively at the man, trying not to get made.

"Jack, don't sit yet, I'd like to go now."

Jack! His name is Jack! What are the odds? Sid turned slightly so he could get a better look at this Jack. Then he saw the beautiful black woman get up and move into the aisle, kissing her Jack and giving his face a light caress as she quickly disappeared into the lavatory. *Could this be my guy? He matches the description. What do I do?* He needed to take a picture of this Jack character while he was waiting for his bride. He pulled out his phone, switched it into selfie mode, made sure it was set to silent, and snapped a photo. But when he looked at it, he could barely make out Jack because of the back light coming in from the airplane's windows. He immediately snapped another one, but it wasn't any better. The black woman came out of the lavatory and once again, flirted with her Jack as she passed him by to retake her seat. "Shit! Shit! Shit!" He whispered angrily shoving his phone back into his pocket. He would have to try again later, when the back light had dissipated.

Hours later, a cabin tone sounded. "Ladies and gentlemen, we are about to begin our descent into Sydney, Australia. Please place your seatbacks upright and place your tray table into the locked position. The flight attendants will be coming around to collect any trash. Thank you."

There was a sound of seats being re-positioned, the clatter of tray tables being lifted, and the chatter of excited tourists who were exhausted by the lengthy flight.

Sid was still trying to figure out how to get another photo of Jack.

Twenty minutes later, another cabin tone was heard. "Ladies and gentlemen, please make sure your seatbelts are fastened, while storing any baggage in the overhead compartments or under the seat ahead of you. Keep in mind that items in the overhead compartments may have shifted during flight. Thank you."

Damn! Time is running out.

As the aircraft descended, Sid heard the comforting sound of the landing gear. The aircraft had a firm touchdown on the runway, and the passengers cheered and clapped, including Sid and Janice.

"Hey Honey, why don't you take a picture of us on the plane? I could post it once we have Wi-Fi."

Here was his chance. "Great idea." Sid pulled his phone out and took a few photos of him and his wife and a few of the man behind him, who was now standing waiting to exit the plane. He clicked a few times and looked at the shots. *Perfect!* "Got some good ones, Hon."

"Great I'll see them after we get off."

Sid stored his phone in his pocket and began to collect his stuff. As the people moved ahead of him, he followed, ensuring that his wife was behind him. He was extremely protective of her. God forbid something would happen to her; he wouldn't be able to live.

Once off the jetway and inside the terminal, Sid tried to keep an eye on Jack and his wife. But in the crush of passengers trying to get to baggage claim, they both disappeared from his sight.

"Crap." he said softly.

"What's crap?" Janice had heard him perfectly.

"Oh, nothing. the restrooms are far away." *Nice save,* he thought.

"Oh, yes, so come on, step on it," Janice ordered as she increased her pace, pulling her carry-on behind her.

Sid shook his head and tried to keep up. "I need to walk more."

When he arrived in the men's room, he rolled his baggage into the largest stall he could find. He sat down, pulled out his phone, and went through his photos. He found some that needed to be discarded, but some were very good. He deleted the bad ones and moved the good ones into a folder so he could show them to the Australian police when he had a chance. He left the ones he took of him and Janice in the photo gallery, put his phone away, finished his business, and went out to meet up with Janice.

"Okay, here we go. Ready?"

"Oh yes but first, I need a nap."

Janice burst out laughing. "Yes, me too."

~~~~~~

Jack and Adaora began their honeymoon in the thriving metropolis of Sydney, the pride of the Southern Hemisphere, with the best beaches and landmarks. They launched their vacation by enjoying a show at the iconic Opera House, then enjoying the cobblestone streets and the nineteenth century buildings on the Rocks, the thriving lifestyle at the Darling Harbour, and ended with a visit to the Royal Botanic Garden.

"Oh, Jack, this city is awesome! I've never seen anything like it."

"It is unique for sure, but I'm realizing it's too busy for me. I prefer Melbourne."

"Okay, well, we're headed there next. Right?"

"Yes, but don't you want to visit the beaches?"

"Oh, yes, of course." she pulled her phone out of her purse and looked up the beaches. "Says here that the Bondi Beach and Marley Beach are the best beaches in this area."

"Good. That's where we'll go, then, love."

"Jack, I'd love to meet your parents."

Where did that come from? "No, you don't." he snapped at her.

"Why? Don't you want them to meet me?"

"No, I don't!" he raised his voice.

"But why Jack? I don't understand why you're hesitant. I'd love to meet them. They can't be that bad. Please try..."

He slapped her hard with his left hand while he kept his right hand on the wheel. "Just drop it!" his tone was low and angry.

Rubbing her cheek, Adaora turned away from Jack so he wouldn't see her tears. She tried to make sense of his outburst, but she couldn't. She realized that she was alone in this foreign land and as such, she had no power. She couldn't even go to the authorities. She didn't know anyone who could help her. And now, she didn't even know her own husband!

A few hours later he asked, "You all right, Love?"

Adaora turned to give her husband a huge fake smile. "Yes, I'm fine," she said meekly.

Jack was impressed at how his new wife adapted quickly to his authority. He just gave her a life lesson; he was the head of the household, and *HE* would decide where they went and who they visited, and how much money they spent.

~~~~~~

By the time Janice was satisfied with her dillydallying in Sydney, Sid was about ready to fly home. But, of course, he couldn't dare tell her that. So, like a good husband, he followed her to the famous Opera House, the Harbour Bridge, the Rocks, the Darling Harbour, and the Royal Botanic Garden. Just before they took on the eight-hour road trip to Melbourne, Janice wanted to get some beach time in, so, they visited both Coogee Beach and Manly Beach. After all the touring and fun times, it was time to get down to business.

Chapter 14

"That was a great week. Thanks, Honey." Janice snuggled close to her husband and kissed him on the cheek.

"Anything for my favorite girl."

"You're lying through your teeth, but I appreciate that. You're the best husband."

Sid found a cool radio station that played the oldies, but as he drove out of Sydney it faded away.

Janice broke the silence. "Okay, now let's talk shop. Where are we going first?"

"Well, I'd like to visit Nora's grandparents' place. I have some photos to show them, and I have to tell them about their daughter. I don't think they know."

"Oh, good call."

"That's gonna be tough."

"I'll be right there." She slid her hand up and down his forearm.

"Thanks Hon."

There was a bit of silence as if to honor Fausta's memory.

"Then it's off to Melbourne."

"Right. We're meeting the Welbys, right?"

"Yes, seems like they were investigating Jack before he left for the states, and they informed the Melbourne P.D. But nothing ever came out of that."

"That's odd, right?"

"Yes, but Jack changed his name and got a fake passport. He was right under our noses the whole time, and nobody ever knew."

"Well, until we met Nora, we had no clue about the situation. We were in Mississippi while all this was going on in Florida."

"True." Sid was beginning to feel discouraged.

"Cheer up, Sid. If anyone's going to solve this crime, it'll be you."

"I don't know, Hon. this one's a toughie."

A few hours later, Sid knocked on the Benitos' door.

An almost stereotypical-looking Italian man opened the door. "Oh, Mr. Daniels?" he asked with a slight accent.

"Yes, and this is my wife, Janice."

The men shook hands.

"Nice to meet you both. Please come in, come in."

They entered a small, modest bungalow decorated with a beach flair.

"Such a pretty place you have here, Mrs. Benito," Janice complimented.

"Thank you. But please. I'm Gabriella. Mrs. Benito was my mother-in-law." They all chuckled at that ice breaker. "Nice to meet you both, Gabriella continued." She guided everyone into the living room. "Please, have a seat."

"I'll make some coffee, or would you prefer espresso?"

"I'll have the coffee, she prefers espresso."

"Bene! I'll make both, then." she disappeared into the kitchen and re-appeared with a tray of biscotti. "I just made these. Please help yourself."

"Nice neighborhood. How long have you been here?" Sid asked.

"Ever since that scoundrel threatened us. We got so scared, we sold the house back in Melbourne and moved here."

"We had retired anyway, so it was a good time to make the move."

Sid pulled out a small notepad and pen. "Please tell me about the last encounter with Jack."

As Vincenzo told the story, Sid scribbled.

"I'm sorry you had to go through that." Try as she might, Janice couldn't imagine experiencing that sort of trauma.

Sid cleared his throat. "This is very hard for me, but I must be very blunt, here. We have very good reason to believe that he killed your daughter."

"What?" Vincenzo's mouth fell open.

"Oh, no!" Gabriella shot up and scrunched her hair with her hands, "No, la mia Fausta! No!" she picked up a photo of Fausta and Jack, what seemed like a wedding photo. "Murderer!" she threw the frame on the wooden floor, smashing it to pieces. She hid her face in her hands and wept. Vincenzo sat next to her and placed his arm around her. "What about our granddaughter, Nora?"

"She's fine. She graduated university and is an engineer now." Janice pulled out her phone and searched for the photos she had intended to show the elderly couple. "Here, this is Nora with our son SJ. They have been together for a few years now. She's like a daughter to us." she handed the phone to Vincenzo.

"Oh, my, Gabri, look at our granddaughter. Isn't she beautiful?"

Gabriella wiped her eyes with her handkerchief, took the phone, and suddenly the sadness melted and gave way to joy. "Oh, she's beautiful!" she placed the phone next to her heart and then she swiped the screen to the next photo. "Such a handsome couple." She handed the phone back to Janice.

"Thank you. we are extremely proud of both of them. They have accomplished a lot in their lives."

"So, tell me, how did it happen?"

Sid proceeded to tell the story of Fausta's presumed death, how Nora heard the entire ordeal while sitting in her closet, and he told her about Carly's mysterious death.

"He's rotten to the core, he is." Vincenzo was sweeping up the broken pieces of picture frame. "I always knew there was something not right in his head, especially after what happened at our old home."

"Is that why you moved here?" Sid asked.

"Oh yes, I was terrified, and I wanted out. I found the most hidden senior village. We sold the house and moved before Jack would be out of jail."

"So, when was the last time you saw your daughter."

"Just a few days before that animal came pounding on our door." Vincenzo said.

"Yes, she came to say goodbye. We did not realize at the time that she was pregnant. She never said a word to us." Gabriella was getting emotional again. She wiped the corner of her eye with her apron. "I never thought it would be the last time I would see her."

"Did you hear from her after that?"

"Oh yes." Gabriella got up and went to the kitchen. "She would mail us postcards every year with photos of her and Nora, or sometimes just Nora." she removed all the postcards from the fridge and brought them into the living room. "Here, these are all the postcards we ever got from Fausta." she spread them out on the coffee table.

Janice picked up a few. "Oh my, your daughter was a beautiful woman!" she flipped through the photos. "And Nora was such a lovely child."

"Yes, we treasure these postcards because it is all we have of them." Vincenzo began to weep quietly. "And now she's gone." he sniffled as he pulled out his handkerchief.

Sid was not one to get emotional, but this was too much. He got up and left the room.

"I wanted to leave this for later on, but I think you need it right now." Janice swiped her phone and searched for a video. She set it in landscape mode and handed it to Gabriella. "Go ahead, hit play."

Nora and SJ appeared on the screen. "Ciao Nonna and Nonno, it's me Nora, your granddaughter. I want you to meet my boyfriend SJ. He means everything to me. I promise you both that I'll be visiting you very soon. But for now, I'm sending all my love and kisses..." Nora blew kisses into the camera. "And remember, I love you very much, and so did Mom. She always wanted to come back and visit but..." her mood became more somber. "Anyway, I love you, okay?

Don't ever forget that." Both grandparents were weeping and blowing kisses back at the phone's screen.

SJ continued. "And Mr. and Mrs. Benito, please know that I love your granddaughter very much and I will protect her with my life. Be sure of that. Goodbye and we'll chat soon." The screen went dark.

"Oh, thank you! Thank you and God bless you! You made two old people very happy," Gabriella exclaimed through her tears.

"I figured you needed that, and Nora told me that you can FaceTime her whenever you want. She's going to do her best to answer you, okay."

"You have given us so much hope. Bless you." Vincenzo got up and hugged them both.

"It was our pleasure." Sid sat down again. "Now, I need to know if he has any relatives in Melbourne, or any friends that you know of."

The Benitos looked at each other. "I'm not sure. I think his parents are still alive, but I'm not sure."

"Do you have an address for them?"

"Wait, I may have something written down in an old address book...wait." Vincenzo made his way to the back of the bungalow.

"You know, we got a phone call once, too."

"You did? Tell us about it." Sid flipped a page on his little notepad.

"Fausta called and that's when we talked to Nora for the first time. It was exciting but come to think of it, it was the last time I heard my daughter's voice." she sniffled.

"What did you talk about?"

"She wanted to know if we had seen or heard from Jack, and we told her what happened at our old house. But we assured her that he could not find us now. And he never did, thank God. But he did find her." she sat back down and began to cry again. "I still can't believe he killed my baby girl. How could he do that? They were in love. I don't understand it."

Vincenzo walked into the room with a small, worn out booklet. "I found his parents' information."

"Can you read it to me? I'll take notes."

"Diego and Giacinta Rinaldi, 701 Drummond Street, Melbourne, Victoria. I have their number too."

"Sure, I'll take that too."

"613934788552."

"Got it." Sid shut his notebook and slid it into his jacket pocket.

"Please, stay for espresso and biscotti. I made them fresh when you were on your way."

"Oh, how marvelous. I bake biscotti too. We will have to compare notes."

"Of course. Ha-ha." the little Italian Nonna seemed in a better frame of mind.

"We have a long drive, Hon." Sid was not really in the mood for socializing.

"It will only be another half hour." Janice gave Sid a stern look and patted the couch next to her.

That was his clear signal not to be his rude self. "Fine." He reluctantly sat next to his wife.

"Good man." she patted his knee.

About five minutes later, Gabriella entered the living room with a large tray with four espresso cups and a small mountain of biscotti.

Almost two hours later, Sid and Janice were finally getting into their rental when Sid walked back to the house. "I'll be right back."

The Benitos were still waving goodbye when Sid returned, holding up his phone.

As he approached, he asked: "I almost forgot. Is this him?" he moved the phone closer so the couple could get a good look at the photo.

"It's dark but...yes...yes it looks like Jack. Of course, he's older in this picture but yes, it is him, for sure."

"Where did you take this picture?" Vincenzo asked.

"Believe it or not, he and his new wife were sitting right behind us on the flight to Sydney."

"So, he's in Australia too?"

"Seems like it."

"That's incredible." Gabriella zoomed in to get a closer look at the photo. "You are some detective, Sid."

"But how did you figure it out?" Vincenzo took one more look at the photo and returned the phone to Sid.

"I had a hunch, is all." but as he turned to go back to the car, he felt a hand holding his arm.

"Please, Mr. Sid. Find this lowlife and bring him to justice."

"I'll do my best, Mrs. Benito, I promise."

Gabriella gave Sid a warm hug while Vincenzo shook his hand vigorously.

"What was that all about?" Janice asked as Sid started the engine.

"Here. Take a look at my phone." he handed his phone to his wife.

"What am I looking at?" she swiped the phone and found herself looking at the photo of Jack taken on the airplane.

"Well, do you recognize him?"

She expanded the photo and squinted. "No. Who is he?"

"That's Jack."

"What?" she moved the phone back and forth to see if she recognized him.

"Where did you take this picture?"

"On our flight to Sydney."

"What? I never saw him! How did you figure it out?"

"I heard him talking with his wife. She was the black woman sitting next to him and they were sitting right behind us, by the way."

"You're kidding, right?"

"Nope."

"Are you sure he's Jack?"

"Yes, they just confirmed it," pointing back at the Benitos.

"Oh my God! He was sitting right behind us! What are the odds?"

"Slim to none."

"Sid, you do know that this proves that you still got it, right?"

Sid nodded and smiled. He was so close.

Chapter 15

The Sheraton was in the middle of the business district and only a few blocks away from the Melbourne East Police Station. It was only an eight-minute walk but somehow, it took over a half hour. Janice was mesmerized by all the different restaurants from around the world, to the tiny boutique shops, to the coffee shops, and her most favorite— the bookstore. She was determined to buy some books from independent (indie) Aussie authors. She went in, asked some questions, and walked out with half a dozen paperbacks by different indie authors, all from Australia. They had traveled to a few countries throughout their lifetime, and she always supported local authors. She made sure they signed the books she bought. She figured that one day, they might become famous, and then she would have a unique, signed copy in her possession. Besides, those stories just seemed better than the big-name authors, especially in her preferred genres. Janice figured it was because the indies wrote from the heart, not for the love of money.

A noticeably young Australian constable greeted them as they approached the front desk. "May I be of assistance?"

"Certainly. My name is Sid Daniels, and this is my wife, Janice. We have an appointment to meet with Inspector Welby."

"Which Welby sir?"

"Both, actually. We'd like to speak with both. They are waiting for us."

The Constable picked up a phone and dialed a number. "Mr. and Mrs. Daniels here to see you sir." then a pause. "Very well sir." he hung up the phone and pointed to the entry door. "Right this way, please."

Sid and Janice followed the young officer into an office located down the hallway. Like American police stations, this squad room was abuzz with officers, suspects, and other people.

"Mr. and Mrs. Daniels, pleasure to meet you both." A middle-aged man in a shirt and tie reached out to shake Sid's hand. The detective was tall and muscular, with a slight bulge around his midsection. His eyes were bright green, almost piercing. His blonde hair was threaded with some silver here and there, His shield hung from his neck.

"Inspector Welby, I presume?" Sid shook his hand.

"Yes." Then he reached for Janice's hand. "Please, have a seat. Can I get you anything?"

"Oh, no, we're fine. Thanks for asking." Janice looked around the office and noted a bunch of awards and citations. "This is quite remarkable."

"Thank you. They call us the Welby Duo," a female voice said. April strode in, closed the door, and reached out to shake the couple's hands. "Nice to meet both of you." she was almost as tall as her husband. Her curves had turned into plumpness over the years, but she was still a stunning woman with a thick mane of auburn hair only lightly touched with white. She had sparkling gray eyes. Her features were typical of an Anglo-Saxon princess who had grown into a Queen. She made herself comfortable on the side of his huge metal desk.

"Yes. ever since we decided to get married, our case-solving efforts became doubly effective. Best thing we ever did was get married." She gazed at her crime-fighting husband with loving eyes.

"Now, April, I don't think they traveled all the way from Florida to hear about our relationship. Am I correct?"

"If it has to do with solving the case, then yes." Sid's response was diplomatic, trying not to hurt anyone's feelings.

Janice smacked him in the upper arm. "Always a smart-ass, this guy!"

They all laughed, and hence the ice was broken.

Kevin opened a side drawer, pulled out a manila folder, and placed it in front of Sid. "Here you are mate. This is what we have on Jack."

Sid opened the file and flipped through it quickly, getting a whiff of the character of his subject. He paused when he got to Jack's first victim. "Who was this woman?" he pointed at a photo of the body, snapped minutes after they arrived on scene.

"That is Jessica Richards." Kevin tapped his finger on the photo.

"She was connived into believing Jack, but once he got what he wanted, that's what he did to her." April gave more details.

"That's horrendous!" Janice felt queasy.

"Mrs. Daniels, would you like to get some coffee?"

"No, April, I'd like to get some air." she got up. "Can you show me out, please?"

"I'll be right back." April left the room with Janice following close behind.

"I'm sorry about my wife. She's not a cop. She came on this trip for moral support and to do some touristing."

"I understand. April will take good care of her."

"May I have a copy of his case file?"

"Certainly. I'll have the Constable make copies for you."

"Great. So now, I have something to show you." Sid pulled his phone out, searched for the infamous photo, and showed it to Kevin.

"What? Is that Jack?"

"I believe so."

"Where was this taken?"

"On the flight to Sydney."

Kevin zoomed the photo. "Looks like him, all right." he gave the phone back to Sid, "Would you mind texting me that?"

"Sure, what's your number?"

A few minutes later, the photo was on Kevin's phone. "Brilliant!" he fiddled with his phone and the printer started up. "I'm printing it. It's probably the only photo we're going to have to work with."

"Good idea. I'm old school, too; I prefer pushing paper."

"All right, now. According to this photo," he picked up the printed photo from the printer, "Jack is in Australia."

"Yes, he and his new wife were on the plane sitting right behind us."

"That's incredible, mate." he placed the newly printed photo into the manila folder. "What made you suspicious that it could be him?" Kevin was astounded at the coincidence.

"Well, before I left, I went to our Melbourne Police Department and had a chat with Detective Terrance Bouchuroix who was engaged to Fausta's best friend, Carly McIntyre, who also died under suspicious circumstances. Around the time of Fausta's kidnapping, Carly gave the police all the photos that Fausta had kept in her secret place in the hopes of finding her."

"So, Fausta wasn't killed in 2008, then?"

Sid decided it was the moment to give Inspector Welby a copy of the Melbourne, Florida police case file. "No. Initially, it was thought that she was kidnapped, but after years of searching the case was filed away as a cold case presumed homicide, since they never found the body. It's all in there." He handed the file to Kevin.

The inspector briefly skimmed the file. "Can I keep this?"

"Yes, this is an official copy of the case file."

"Thanks Mate." he closed the file and placed it inside his file on Jack. "This bloke is a real piece of work. We almost got 'im, but he got away just in time." he tapped on the file. "But now, we have a good chance of finding 'im, we do." He picked up the phone's handset. "I'll bet he's in Melbourne right now, probably visiting some of his hoodlum friends."

"That's what criminals do; they go back to the scene of the crime. It's fairly common."

"Constable, come in here, please."

Not a minute went by and the young Constable who had greeted them at the front desk walked in.

"Yes, sir."

"Here, take this photo, scan it, and put it in the system. then issue a BOLO for Jack Reynolds or Giacomo Rinaldi. Got it?"

"Yes sir, I'm on it." the young man turned on his heels and as he was about to leave, Kevin's voice stopped him.

"Oh, before I forget, make color copies of all the items in this folder please?" he handed the Constable his file on Jack.

"Yes, sir, right away sir." before turning again, he waited a couple of seconds to see if Kevin was done. Then he saluted and went about his way.

"So, let me ask you something."

"Sure."

"When you found out that Jack was in Florida, why didn't you contact Melbourne PD?"

"We did. We sent an international criminal request, but we never received any response."

"Yes, that was unfortunate."

"So, tell me about Carly. What happened to her?"

"Oh, she died of a supposed car accident, but Detective Bouchuroix wasn't convinced. But because no actual evidence was found, her case was closed as an accident."

"Ah, bummer."

"Indeed. But I'm not convinced it was a murder though."

"How so?"

"Well, in my opinion, too many years had passed since the kidnapping of Fausta. You see, Fausta was abducted in 2008 but Carly had her accident in 2019. Why the long wait?"

"Yeah, I agree. If he wanted vengeance, he would have taken care of Carly immediately after Fausta." Kevin looked through the documents Sid gave him. "So, you never found Fausta's body?"

"Nope. Melbourne PD searched for almost ten years but at a certain point, the case went cold because they never found a body."

"Ah, I see."

Sid noticed the wheels spinning in the inspector's brain. "Penny for your thoughts."

"Ummmm....you guys still have the death penalty, right?"

"Yes, I believe the state of Florida still has it, yes. Why do you ask?"

"I was thinking that if you catch Jack, we could file for extradition. But on second thought, the bloke may get the needle, so perhaps it's best if you catch him, you can take care of him, if you know what I mean." he gave Sid a knowing smile.

"Makes sense."

"Good then it's settled. If we find 'im, he goes to the US. If you find 'im, he stays there. Good?"

Sid got up. "You may have to come to the US and testify."

"Gladly, mate." he extended his hand.

Sid nodded as they shook hands.

"Let me walk you out."

April and Janice were waiting for the men to come out.

"You take care, now."

"Kevin, are you going to let these nice Americans leave without going to our favorite place?"

Kevin was embarrassed. His cheeks turned bright red. "Sorry, Luv, you're right." he turned to Sid and Janice. "Do you have some time to join us for dinner this evening? It's on us."

Sid and Janice looked at each other.

"Sure, why not?" Janice jumped in ahead of Sid, knowing that he would politely decline.

April turned to the couple. "Have you been to Giuseppe's Trattoria?"

"No, we haven't eaten in Melbourne yet."

"Excellent!"

"Where are you staying?" April asked.

"At the Sheridan."

"Okay, Sid, we'll be there around eight. Is that okay?"

"Yes, of course. We'll be waiting."

~~~~~~

Around five minutes after eight, a dark gray Honda pulled up to the main entrance of the hotel. Both April and Kevin got out of the car as the Americans walked out of the hotel.

"Wow, you guys look amazing," Janice remarked.

The Aussie couple had shed their work clothes and now looked like a normal couple, dressed up for a night on the town.

"Thanks!"

"Shall we?" Kevin opened the door.

As Janice got in the back, there was a young lady, who was the spitting image of April—but much younger "Well, who do we have here?"

"Mum, you were right, they're dope!"

"May I introduce you to our daughter Melody?"

Melody, in the middle, was joined by Janice on her left and Sid on her right.

"Well, hello there, Melody. I'm Sid." he shook her hand.

"What a lovely name you have. I'm Janice." it was Janice's turn to shake Melody's hand.

Kevin started the car and began making his way down the clean Melbourne streets.

"Are you both cops?" the excitement was bursting out of her pores.

"We're not actually. He's retired and I'm just his wife."

The young lady must have been no older than sixteen, with short boyish-cut hair and the same features as her mother. "Oh, bummer."

"Now, Melody, don't be rude."

"Oh, it's fine." Janice was enjoying this hyper teenager.

"When I graduate, I'm going to the States."

"You are? How exciting!"

"Yeah, I've got three more years still, but I'd go now if I could."

"Do you want to study in the US, Melody?"

"Oh yeah, I do." itching to tell the rest of her plans.

"What do you want to study?"

"Criminal justice. And then I want to become an American cop!"

Sid smiled and nodded. He did not want to be the one to tell her that she had to be an American citizen to become   a   police   officer.

Chapter 16

Melbourne, Florida

Sid told Terrance everything he had learned "Down Under" and gave him the file that Inspector Welby had given him.

While Terrance studied the Aussie folder, Sid looked around the cubicle and noticed a photo that was partially hidden by some kind of chart. Sid got up and reached for it. "May I?"

Terrance nodded and returned to the file.

It was a photo taken with Carly on the beach. It looked like a Glamour Shots picture because of the quality. "Nice shot. When was it taken?"

Terrance looked up, blinking a few times to clear away the tears that were building. "Back in 2019...about a month before her acc..."

"Sorry, man, I should've left it alone." He tried to pin it back up where it was, but it fell on the pile of folders.

Terrance picked it up and stared at it for a minute or so. "Good times." He waved the photo in the air. "She had finally agreed to marry me." he rubbed the tears from his eyes. "I failed her, Sid." he opened the top drawer, looked at the photo one more time and gently placed it inside. "I need to get this guy, fast. I want answers!" His anger showed through.

"I couldn't agree more."

"All right, I've put out a BOLO on him and I've transmitted the photo you took to all L.E. agencies in this area..." he paused a moment on Jack's photo. "By the way, great shot. What are the odds that you guys were on the same flight..." he switched to a different screen. "That reminds me. I requested the passenger lists for both flights, but it looks like they never arrived in Melbourne International. Damn!"

"Christ, what the hell?"

"I know, right. Geez!"

"Well, wait a minute, they were on their honeymoon so they may have met up with friends or relatives in Los Angeles. Check all the flights that left from LAX with both of them on the roster. You may just get lucky."

Terrance's mood changed. He gently punched Sid on his left shoulder. "Nice job!"

"Don't mention it." Sid stifled a wince. He felt the punch, but he didn't want Terrance to think he was a sissy.

Terrance went back at his PC and started punching the keys with excitement. "We're gonna get this piece of crap, I can feel it."

~~~~~~

Adaora entered the construction place in Los Angeles with Jack by her side followed by Enrique who was the Executive Chef while the new location of Passione di Pasta was in construction.

"This is the entrance." He spread his arms. "And this is the dining room. Big, huh?"

"It's huge." Adaora exclaimed while Jack just nodded. He was liking the idea of moving to L.A. It would bring him much closer to home.

"How long before this place is ready?" Adaora asked.

"Oh, it will be at least six months, between permits and other bureaucracy." Enrique would have wanted to open in half that time, but California was vastly different than Florida when it came to regulations on the hospitality business.

"All right, well, let me know when I can start making arrangements to move here."

"Definitely. I would say give yourself about a month to prepare."

"Okay mate, g'day." Jack shook his hand. "Come on Darlin', let's go."

Adaora hooked her arm into her husband's and walked out with him. He could tell she was enthusiastic about moving to L.A. and opening this new location. This would bring her into a managerial position and the pay would be much more than in Florida.

"Too bad it's going to take so long but just think, we'll be living in L.A. don't you love that?"

"Yeah, I'll be closer to home in a way."

"So, you're on board then?"

"Yeah, I am actually." he put his arm around her shoulders.

"Oh, Jack, I'm so happy right now."

"Me too, Luv, me too."

They stopped to kiss each other under the Los Angeles sunshine that was trying to filter through the smog that had intensified with the wildfires still raging in the San Bernardino mountains.

Jack floated an idea. "So, listen. How about we rent a car and drive back to Melbourne?"

"That's a long haul, Baby."

"Yes, I know, but I've always wanted to drive on route 66. Besides, I've never been anywhere other than Florida. I'd love to see the rest of the US. Whaddya ya say, Luv?" he wanted to avoid getting on a plane and going through security over and over. He was getting tired of being scrutinized.

She threw her hands in the air. "Oh, what the hell."

"Good girl!"

A couple of days into their road trip, Adaora had an idea. "Hey Jack, our rent is due when we get back, right?"

"Yes, Luv." he lowered the volume of the radio, as a courtesy.

"Why don't we empty the place, put our stuff in storage, and we could live with my mom while the restaurant is being finished."

"That's brilliant!" his wife just gave him the perfect opportunity to go into hiding again. He didn't have his name on the lease, but now that they were married the landlord would probably require him to be on it. Living with his mother-in-law was not going to be easy, but it would bring him a desired level of incognito. He loved her more and more each day.

"Good, I'm glad you agree." she pulled her phone out. "I'm going to call mom to arrange the whole thing."

A malicious grin came over Jack's face. Once he was back in L.A. he would be scot-free. He looked over at his wife who was talking away with mom, wondering if she was able to read his mind.

~~~~~~

Sid walked into the Indian River Coffee Company where Terrance was waiting to brief him. Sid was more comfortable meeting him in a public place rather than at the police station. He didn't want to step on anyone's toes, especially since he had no jurisdiction in Florida. Not that he had jurisdiction anywhere since he'd retired, but he still felt like he should stay below the radar and work on the case privately.

"Hey Sid."

They shook hands.

"Terrance. Did you order yet?"

"Nope, your turn this time."

"Okay, got it. I'll be right back." Sid got up, went to the counter and ordered their usuals; two black coffees. He waited only a couple of minutes, and with the piping hot mugs in his hands he placed them on their table and took his seat.

"So, any news?"

"Nope. It's like they disappeared off the face of the earth."

"Did you check their address?"

"Yep. The landlord claims they never returned after their honeymoon."

"Jesus!"

"I don't get it. Where did they go? I know for a fact that they landed in LAX."

"Well, I hate to break it to ya, but they could be anywhere in the US right now and finding them is going to be like finding a needle in a haystack." Frowning, Sid took a sip of the hot liquid.

Terrance also sipped his coffee. He shook his head and closed his eyes. "You know, Sid, I'm really getting tired of this. It's been three weeks and we're getting nowhere."

"Don't give up. You can't give up, man, you can't. Have faith."

"I know but it's been years and it seems like we start to get close and then he disappears."

Sid was just as frustrated as Terrance was. He texted every day since they returned from Australia, and every day the return text was the same.

No news.

"Hey man, I hear ya, but you can't give up. We can't give up. We have to keep a positive attitude."

"I know. I know." he shook his head.

"Hey, why don't you come over Saturday. The kids are barbequing."

"Sure, why not. I need a distraction. Thanks man, I'll be there."

"Okay, come around four." Sid got up.

"Yeah, see ya man."

As he drove home, Janice called him and asked if he could bring a pizza home for dinner since she didn't feel like cooking.

"Sure Hon. I'm in the vicinity of Napoli Pizza. The usual?"

"You know it."

"Okay, I should be home around seven."

"Thanks Sid. I appreciate it."

He turned into the parking lot and backed his Ranger into his favorite spot away from the front of the restaurant. It was an old habit from his police days. He walked in and walked straight for the register where a heavily pierced teenager was waiting to take his order.

"What can I get you?"

"Sixteen-inch meat-lover please."

"You got it."

"How long will it be?" he gave her his card.

"About twenty minutes." she swiped his card and gave him the bill to sign.

"Okay." he gave the signed bill back to her. As he placed his wallet in his pocket, the same teenager picked up a large pizza and set it down on a stand at a table where three people were seated. Two black women and a white man.

Holy cow! It's him! It's Jack!

Sid blinked and rubbed his eyes! He could not believe what he was seeing! He stared at them, but when Jack made eye contact Sid looked at his watch. *What do I do now?* He looked at Jack again who went back to his conversation with the two women. Sid walked out of the shop, pulling his phone out.

"Hey Sid."

"He's here!" he shouted into the phone.

"Who's here? Jack? Is it Jack?" Terrance asked.

"Yes, he's here with his wife and another lady and..."

"Sid, where is here?"

Sid looked inside the window to see if they were still there. "Napoli Pizza."

"What? Where's that?"

"Just north of F.I.T."

"Okay, I'll be there in ten." Terrence got into his car and ran siren-and-lights to get to the pizzeria as quickly as possible.

Sid stayed outside, pacing in circles, while keeping an eye out for Terrance. Only five minutes have gone by, when he heard the siren. But by the time Terrance arrived, Sid's excitement had turned to dismay. He blocked Terrance several yards from the pizzeria.

"What's going on? Why are you blocking my way?"

"I thought of something while I was waiting."

"What?"

"Get out of the car and look like you're interrogating me."

"Sure thing!" Terrance gout out of his car and assumed the interview stance.

"Well, you really can't arrest him." he looked back at Jack, who didn't seem to be moved by the police activity outside.

"What do you mean?"

"Just think about it for a minute." Sid pulled Terrance off to the side where Jack couldn't see them. "All you have on him is circumstantial at best."

"Are you kidding right now? You're kidding, right?"

"No, think about this. All we have are some files from Australia that suspect it may be him. Then we have Nora who claims to have seen him, but she only saw him from behind. No facial. We have his voice but that's not going to hold up in court." Sid moves away from Terrance allowing him to go into the pizzeria. "Go on...go in. Arrest him. But what are the charges? I promise you, the State Attorney won't even take this to a judge for a warrant. Tell me I'm wrong."

Terrance went to the driver's side of the cruiser. "Jeez Sid, you're a real buzz-kill, you know that?"

"Perhaps. But if we get this guy, it's got to be the right way. Otherwise, he walks. Is that what you want?"

Terrance climbed into his cruiser. "No, dammit!" He started the engine. "Let me run this by Sabbath. I'll text you later." he drove away, cursing under his breath.

Sid hated those facts as much as Terrance did, but he was not going to give up. He stuck around with the intent to follow Jack to his home and let Terrance know his address. He called Janice to let her know of his discovery.

"Do whatever you need to do Honey."

He loved how understanding she was when it came to his   job...   or   former   job.

Chapter 17

"Sid is right, you know. We've got nothin' on this guy," Sabine Santos stated.

"Correct. BUT! If we put a tail on him, eventually he'll do something wrong." Roth Sabbath looked at Terrance squinting his eyes.

"Right and when we do, we can bring him in." Terrance smiled with this glimmer of hope.

"Good, let's get a uniform on his tail. But he can only stop him if he sees something. We can't risk bringing him in for nothing and having to release him again."

"I just thought of something." Sid rummaged through Jack's file from Australia. "Here it is." he waved a sheet of paper in the air and then gave it to Roth.

As Roth read it, a huge smile came over his face. "We can get him on this." he handed the paper over to Terrance.

Just like Roth, Terrance's face lit up. "Yes, his fake documents."

"That's a third-degree felony." Sabine exclaimed. She knew her Florida statutes quite well.

"Not to mention, his fake passport that he used to get into the US."

"That will get you ten years in prison. Booya!" Sabine gave Terrance a high-five.

"Okay everyone, Operation Melbourne Connection is underway." Roth announced. "Let's get this son of a bitch!"

~~~~~~

Jack was driving up US 1, in his snazzy new Jeep Gladiator, to get to work. He was on cloud nine. After many years, he was made supervisory custodian at F.I.T., and on top of that, Adaora gave him the news of her pregnancy test: positive.

"I'm going to be a father?" he couldn't believe his joy.

"Yes, my love you are." she was glowing.

He picked her up and twirled her around the room. Then he realized that she could get dizzy or something and damage the baby. "Oh, I'm sorry, Luv..." he gently put her down. "Are you okay?" and patted her tummy.

"Yes, Jack, I'm fine." she gently pulled him toward the bed. "Come, let me show you just how fine I am."

Jack loved it when she took charge. Suddenly his thoughts were interrupted by a cruiser following behind him who was flashing his lights to pull over. *Was I speeding? I don't think so.* He pulled over, but the police officer didn't get out of the cruiser for a good minute or more.

"Good morning, sir. May I have your license and registration please?" The officer kept his right hand ready to pull his weapon if Jack tried anything funny.

"G'day officer. What's this about?"

The officer had been instructed not to spook him. "Your left turn signal doesn't seem to be working."

Whew. He pulled out the requested documents and handed them over to the officer. "There you are." A signal was nothing. He would be on his way in no time.

"Thank you, sir. I'll be right back. Just sit tight."

The young officer did as he had been instructed. He ran Jack's license through the system and, sure enough, it came back as no record found. The insurance was in his wife's name, along with the registration of the Jeep. The officer called for backup, and in several minutes two other cruisers arrived and blocked Jack from driving away. This had to be handled meticulously and without a glitch. Just as the other two cruisers positioned themselves on the front and left side of Jack's Jeep, the young officer approached him.

"I'm afraid I'm going to have to ask you to step out of your vehicle, sir." The officer opened the door of the Jeep.

Jack was taken aback. "But why officer..." he realized that he couldn't go anywhere. He was stuck. "...what did I do?"

"Please turn around, sir."

"But I didn't do anything! What's going on here? I demand to know! All this drama for a turn signal?" he raised his arms so the officer couldn't cuff him.

The other two officers were pulling his arms down and behind his back so he could be handcuffed. "Keep still, sir, keep still." Jack felt something being pressed into his side. "If you continue to resist, we'll be forced to Taser you."

Jack did as he was told, realizing that the jig was up. "I demand to know what I'm being arrested for."

"You are being charged with possession of a forged driver's license. You have the right to remain silent. Anything you say can and will be used against you in a court of law. You have the right to an attorney. If you cannot afford an attorney, one will be provided for you. Do you understand the rights I have just read to you?"

From all the police shows he watched on American television; he knew that he had to not say a word going forward. "Yes."

"With these rights in mind, do you wish to speak to me?"

The other two officers gently sat him in the back of the young officer's cruiser.

"No," was all that Jack said while his thoughts were how he was going to tell his wife that his entire existence was fake.

~~~~~~

Detective Bouchuroix walked into the "Passione di Pasta" restaurant. Adaora greeted him at the entrance since she was the head hostess.

"Hello, will it be only you today, sir?" she gave Terrance a big smile.

"I need to speak with you." he flashed his badge. "Is there anywhere we can talk privately?"

Her grandiose smile disappeared. "What's this about?"

"It's about your husband."

"My husband?"

"Yes. Now, we can either talk here or you can come down to the station with me."

Dreading the latter option, she waved him to follow her into a small office on the north side of the restaurant. "We can talk here."

Terrance stayed on his feet while she preferred to sit.

"What's going on? Is Jack okay?"

"He's fine but he's in custody."

"Custody? For what?"

"Driving with a forged driver's license."

"What? No way! I can't believe it."

"Well, it's true. Now I need to ask you a few questions."

231

She pressed her lips together. "Do I need a lawyer?"

"I don't think so. It's just a few questions."

She shook her head. "Sure, go ahead."

"Do you know where your husband was born?"

"Uh...yeah...he's Australian."

"Okay, so do you know his real identity?"

She gave him a puzzled look. "Yeah, it's Jack Reynolds."

It was his turn to shake his head. "No, actually his real name is Giacomo Rinaldi."

"Okay, so people change their identity all the time. Nothing wrong with that, right?"

"Yes, people do change their identity, especially when they're running away from a country that has a bounty on them for murder."

"Murder?" she shot up from her seat. "Jack's not a murderer. He's the kindest man I've ever met and he's ga—" She stopped short.

"What?"

He was the father of her baby. A killer was the father of her baby. No way. This isn't happening. "Who did he kill? And where's the evidence?"

Terrance proceeded to take a few photos out of his front jacket pocket. He placed them carefully on the desk. "Jessica Richards. He stabbed her in 2007, near his apartment building in Melbourne Australia, just days before he flew to Florida."

As she sat back down, fearful tears welled in her eyes. She looked at the dead body in the photos. In horror, she covered her mouth with her hand. "B-but why? Why would he do this?"

"To get information." he sat down on the corner of the desk. "Did he ever mention he was married in Australia?"

"Yes, he mentioned his first wife. They didn't get along, so he divorced her and came to Florida for a new start."

Shaking his head, once again, he said; "No, I'm sorry, that's not what happened, according to what our investigation uncovered."

"I guess I should know what really happened, shouldn't I?" she sadly asked, looking down at her wedding ring.

"Are you sure?"

She closed her eyes for a moment and nodded. Tears began streaming down her face.

"Okay, well, in 2008 there was an abduction of a woman. Do you remember that?"

"Yeah, I was a teenager, then, but yes, I remember her face plastered all over the TV and internet, not to mention every traffic light and stop sign."

"Yes, exactly. That was Fausta Benito."

"Yes, I remember her name now." she paused to think. "So, Jack kidnapped her and then killed her?" she asked in a trembling voice.

"Seems like it."

"Well, how do you know it was Jack?"

"We have a witness who heard everything. Her daughter."

"Daughter? The woman who was abducted had a daughter?"

"Yes, she was hiding in the closet when the incident took place. She heard everything."

"She didn't see anything though."

"She was looking through the slats in the closet door. She saw and heard everything."

"What...wait...daughter? So, the girl is Jack's daughter too?" she said as her left hand gently rubbed her lower abdomen.

"Yes, she is, and she's not a girl anymore. She's a grown woman."

"Oh my God, I'm going to be sick...move!" Pushing him out of her way, she left like a bullet and disappeared into the hallway.

Terrance shook his head. He really hated this part of his job, but it had to be done. He looked at his watch while waiting patiently for Adaora to return.

She came in again, sat down and pouted. "So, now what?"

"I have a couple of other questions."

She just shrugged her shoulders.

"Did he ever talk about a Carly McIntyre?"

"No, why? Who's she?"

"She was Fausta's best friend. She brought Fausta to Florida when she found out she was pregnant. She wanted Fausta to be safe because of her pregnancy."

"Why safe?"

"Because he abused her, physically."

"I see." she did notice he had a violent streak, but he had slapped her only that one time, in Australia.

"Was he violent with you?"

"Not all the time. He has a short temper, but he never laid a finger on me." She lied.

"Perhaps he mellowed out throughout the years."

"Well, I've got to get back to work. Can I go?"

"Yes, but I need you to sign this affidavit, first." he pulled out a document with a pen.

"Why?"

"It's a sworn statement that you had nothing to do with Jack's crimes and that he never confessed anything to you. Unless he did; then I'd recommend you get yourself a lawyer."

Her thoughts strayed to that day on her honeymoon when Jack revealed his personality, even if only once. She took the pen and signed the document. "Here." she handed the paper to him, along with the pen. "I don't ever want to see Jack again."

~~~~~~

Roth, Sabine and Jack were sitting in the interrogation room. Jack was restrained to the metal loop on the table with handcuffs. A manila folder was on the table between them. On the other side of the mirror, were Sid and Terrance.

"All right, Mr. Reynolds. Or shall I say Mr. Rinaldi?" Sabine broke the ice.

"Don't know what ya coppers are talkin' about. My name is Jack Reynolds and that's it."

"Really! Well, that's not what your birth certificate says." Roth handed Jack an original of his birth certificate, certified by the Australian authorities. "See the stamp? It's authentic."

"Don't care. Not me."

Roth and Sabine gave each other a knowing glance.

"All right then, how do you explain the fake driver's license and Australian passport?"

Jack shrugged his shoulders while giving them a condescending smirk.

"Well, Jack, if you say you are who you are, then why didn't you get a real passport?"

"Dunno."

"I'm pretty sure you needed to change your identity after you killed Jessica Richards. Right?" Sabine asked.

"I didn' kill anyone."

"No, you did, and then you came to Florida looking for your wife." Roth pulled out their wedding photo and gently slid it between Jack's restrained hands. "What a lovely couple. Isn't that right, Jack?"

Jack's smug expression softened when he saw his wedding picture. He shook his head as tears began to form.

"What did you do with her body, Jack?" Roth came right out and asked, noticing the sudden change in his demeanor.

"I'm not talkin' to you coppers! I know my rights! I've done nothin' wrong!"

The detectives had him removed from the interrogation room and placed him back in the holding cell.

The three men and Sabine met in the hallway.

"What do we do now?" Sabine asked.

"I have an idea." Sid said.

"Shoot." Roth motioned the group to go back into the interrogation room.

"We have one more ace up our sleeve."

"Go on." Sabine didn't sit. She was too irritated to sit still. Instead, she paced back and forth.

"Nora. She heard him saying the same phrase twice." he had everyone's attention. "We can bring her in and have her listen to his voice. She can recognize him. I'm sure of it."

"But Sid, will she be able to recognize him just by listening to his voice? Or will he need to say the exact phrase she heard him say to her mother? 'Cause that's gonna be hard to do." Terrance interjected.

"Let me talk to him. I'll persuade him to repeat that phrase into my recorder," Sabine said.

Sid chimed in. "He's not going to fall for that. He's not you're run of the mill dumbass."

"I know. We can tell him that it's to help convict another Aussie criminal who robbed a bank and all we have is his voice saying that phrase. From what I understand, it's rather common Down Under," Terrance added.

"Do you think he'll fall for that?" Roth asked.

"Only one way to find out." Sabine turned to Terrance. "Write it down for me." she pulled out her pen and notepad and handed it to Terrance.

Terrance wrote it down and gave it back to Sabine.

"All right let's do it." she headed for the holding cell.

"Mr. Reynolds, we need your help." Sabine turned her recorder on along with her charm.

He stood up and went toward them with a smirk. "Oh, ya do?"

"Yes, and we can make it worth your while."

"I'm list'nin'."

"I need you to read this phrase into my recorder so we can use it in another case, an Aussie bank robber that we've been trying to get for a while. This is the only way it will hold up in court." Roth winked at Sabine making sure that Jack didn't notice.

"And what's in it for me?"

"We'll talk to the state attorney and get the counterfeit DL charges dropped."

Jack turned and went to sit down to think. *At least I can get that accusation taken off my record.* "What about the fake passport?"

"So, you're admitting it's fake now?" Roth raised his eyebrow.

"Yeah, yeah, so what can you do about that? I don't want to go back to Australia, man. I've got a baby on the way 'ere."

"Hold on..."

239

Roth and Sabine huddled in a corner of the room and whispered so Jack couldn't hear.

"Okay, Mr. Reynolds, you have a deal."

"Here, let me get this ready." she hit stop and then hit record again. She gave Jack the piece of paper with the phrase on it. "Now, I want you to say it like you're robbing a bank. Let me hear it."

"Gidday darlin'. Well blow me down! Finally found ya slag!"

"Okay, that was good, but I need you to repeat it. But angrier this time."

"Gidday darlin'. Well blow me down! Finally found ya slag!" just as he was asked. "Are we done now?"

Sabine hit the stop button. "Yes, sir we are."

"So, when am I getting released?"

"That's going to take a while. Just hang tight. We're going to the state attorney's office right after we arrest this guy." Roth pointed at Sabine's recorder.

Sid and Terrance were waiting for Roth and Sabine in the hallway.

"Got it!" Roth excitedly exclaimed.

"Now what?" asked Sabine.

"Just like the visual witnesses, we need to line up at least six other potential criminals so Nora can make her choice."

"Well, Sid, where are we going to find five other Aussie males?" Roth asked.

Sid rubbed his forehead with his fingers. This wasn't looking good, and the looks on the faces of the other three detectives confirmed it. "Wait! I've got it." he pulled out his phone. "I'm calling Inspector Welby in Melbourne and..."

"Welby? I don't know any Welby..." Roth stated.

"No, Melbourne Australia. He and his wife, April, are heading the investigation over there. Let me reach out and see what they can do to help us." he checked the time on his phone. "Well, shit, it's five in the morning there right now, so we won't get a response for probably another couple of hours."

"We can hold Jack. No problem," Terrance said.

"Good, okay let me leave a voicemail." Sid dialed the number.

After a few rings, "Welby 'ere."

Sid was surprised. "Inspector Welby, Sid Daniels calling."

Everyone was pleased that Sid's call did not go to voicemail.

"Oh, Sid, how are you?"

"I'm okay, but what are you doing up so early?"

"I'm getting' ready for a run. What's goin' on mate?"

Sid explained in detail what he needed and hung up. "Okay, he's sending an email in a few hours."

"What's going to be in the email?" Terrance asked.

"Oh, you'll see." Sid grinned with satisfaction. He dialed another number. "Nora, it's Sid. Can you give me a call back please? It's quite urgent. Thanks."

~~~~~~

Around ten, Nora walked into the Melbourne PD accompanied by SJ. The front desk officer had been told to expect them. He signed them in and guided them to an interview room. Sid and Terrance came into the room.

"Uncle Terry!" Nora hugged him lovingly. "It's been too long!"

"I know Nora. And you're right, but I've been up to my eyeballs in alligators, working cases."

"So typical." she smiled warmly and sat next to SJ.

Sid and Terrance went into the adjoining room and watched through the one-way window.

Sabine pulled out an audio device and set it in front of Nora. "This lineup is being videotaped. It's extremely important that we do this properly. I want you to listen very closely to my instructions. Okay?"

"Yes," came the timid reply.

"Now, Nora, I'm going to play six different voices that are saying the same exact phrase."

"Yes, you told me this on the phone. It's that famous phrase." she bit her lip.

"Right. But I need you to listen to all of them, one by one, and when I'm done playing the sixth one, then you can tell me if you recognize any of them. The suspect may or may not be in this mix. Got it?"

"Yes."

"Are you ready?"

Nora nodded and hunched over to get closer to the audio device.

"All right. Here we go." Sabine pressed play.

"Voice number one," said a female voice.

"Gidday darlin'. Well blow me down! Finally found ya slag."

Sabine pressed the pause button and looked at Nora. "Good?"

"Yes."

Sabine pressed play again.

"Voice number two."

"Gidday darlin'. Well blow me down! Finally found ya slag!"

Sabine pressed the pause button again. Nora nodded. Sabine pressed play again.

"Voice number three."

"Gidday darlin'. Well blow me down! Finally found ya slag!"

Sabine pressed pause.

"Continue," Nora said.

Sabine pressed play again.

"Voice number four."

"Gidday darlin'. Well blow me down! Finally found ya slag!"

Nora's eyes widened as she covered her mouth with her hand and let out a gasp. Everyone noticed her reaction, and Terrance wrote something in his notepad. SJ put his arm around her shoulder.

"Are you okay?" Sabine asked just to make sure.

"Yes, yes, go on." she answered in a shaky voice.

Sabine pressed play.

"Voice number five."

"Gidday darlin'. Well blow me down! Finally found ya slag!"

Sabine pressed pause. Still shaking, Nora nodded to continue. Sabine pressed play.

"Voice number six."

"Gidday darlin'. Well blow me down! Finally found ya slag!"

Sabine pressed stop. "Did you recognize him?"

"Yes." Nora was still shaking, but she was becoming more collected.

"Okay, I'm going to play them again, but this time I'll play them through until the last one. Ready?"

Nora nodded.

Sabine proceeded to play all six voices again. At voice number four, Nora reacted again. But this time, there was a look of anger on her face.

"Okay Nora, did you recognize any voice?"

"Yes."

"Which one did you recognize?"

"Voice number four."

"Are you certain?"

"Yes, I am. That's definitely him! It's Jack!" Her voice displayed strong determination.

"Okay, so now I need you to sign this affidavit for me." Sabine pulled out a document and handed it to Nora, along with a pen. "I need you to write down which voice it was, and then sign and date on the bottom."

Nora did as she was instructed; she then slid the paper and pen back to Sabine. "So, after all these years, you finally found him?"

"Yes, we did."

"And did Sid help?"

"Yes, Nora, he did."

Nora let out her tears of relief. She hugged everyone in gratitude. "I want to see him," she ordered.

"Um, I don't know if that's possible."

"He killed my mom, and he's my father, too. I want to look into the face of the animal that killed my mom and maybe even Auntie Carly."

"You'll have your chance Nora, but not right now." Terrance stated. He and Sid had re-entered the interview room, since the audio lineup was complete.

"Yes, let them finish their work and then we can arrange for you to meet. Okay?" Sid added.

"Fine." she picked up her purse. "But, as soon as I can, I want to talk to that bastard." and she proudly left the room with SJ right behind her.

"That's one incredibly strong young lady," Sabine remarked.

Sid answered, "Yes, she certainly is."

Chapter 18

Roth unlocked the cell door. "Okay buddy, we're goin'..."

"Am I being released?" Jack asked anxiously.

"Not quite yet." he placed handcuffs on Jack. "We need to have a chat first." Roth pushed him out towards the hallway. "Come on, walk," he ordered angrily.

Jack wondered why the treatment. "I collaborated with you coppers. What do you want now?"

"We're not done yet." he opened the interrogation room and shoved Jack inside. "Now sit." he ordered.

Jack sat and Roth secured him to the loop, like before. "I'll be right back."

Only a few minutes later, Roth and Sabine entered the room and sat in front of Jack. They gently placed two manila folders in front of him. Jack noticed the Melbourne Australia seal on one folder and the Melbourne, Florida seal on the other one. Once again, Terrance and Sid were on the other side of the one-way window.

"Okay Jack, we're not going to waste any more time. We want to resolve this today."

"What more do you want?" he asked with a snooty attitude.

"Let's start from the beginning: we have damning evidence from your hometown police that you killed Jessica Richards." Sabine opened the folder with the Australian seal and slid it under Jack's nose.

"Yeah, so? I'm here and they're down under." He gave a smug shrug of his shoulders.

"So, you're admitting it?"

Jack nodded.

"Is that a yes?"

"Yeah, sure," Jack answered. He was feeling his oats, thinking that these American coppers had nothing on him.

"Great. And do you also admit to buying a fake Australian passport?"

"Yeah, so what?" he asked smugly. He didn't think that all this mattered, now that he had been cooperative with the American police. He was holding them to their word. "You made me a promise, mates, and ya need ta come through."

"In a moment."

Jack slumped in his chair, getting angrier by the minute.

Seth proceeded to open the Melbourne, Florida folder. "Okay, so says here you were seen kidnapping Fausta Benito on August 25th, 2008. Can you confirm that?"

"Her name was Rinaldi, not Benito." Jack snapped angrily.

"Okay, why Rinaldi?" Sabine knew the answer already, but she wanted him to confess.

Jack moved his torso forward. "Because she was my wife, that's why." he peered at the two detectives.

"I'm sorry, I'm confused. Isn't your last name Reynolds?" Sabine asked.

"No, that's a fake name, you idiot! My name is Giacomo Rinaldi, and Fausta was my wife."

"Was? Is that because you killed her?"

"No, I don't know what happened to her."

"Okay, so tell me this; why did you come to the US?"

"I needed a change of scenery, and I was attracted to Melbourne Florida."

"Oh, okay. Another question: do you know Carly McIntyre?"

"Yeah, I do. That whore took my Faussy away from me." he tried to get up, but the cuffs held him down. "She had no right to do that!" His voice became louder and louder, as his temper got shorter and shorter.

"Jack, sit down and calm down!" Roth demanded.

Jack did what he was told, but he was far from calm.

"Jack, you got re-married, right?" Sabine changed the subject.

Jack's demeanor changed at that question. "Yeah, and I got a baby on the way too."

"Well, congrats. Sounds like you have a bright future ahead of you." Sabine's voice dripped with sarcasm.

"Yeah, I do." he smiled that same smug smile he was famous for.

"Well, I hate to tell you this, but Adaora Grant wants nothing to do with you." Sabine pulled out the affidavit and showed it to Jack.

"Grant? Her name is Reynolds. What is with you coppers? Can't you get your names right?"

"Oh, we have her name right, because Reynolds is a fake name, hence making your marriage null and void, according to Florida law you are a single man, and she is a single woman."

"You can't do this! It's my baby!" he stomped his foot so that it was felt by all in the room.

"No, it's not. It's Adaora's baby."

Jack sneered at Sabine.

"Now, Jack, you need to understand that we have so much evidence against you that we could get you the death penalty." Roth said.

Jack's eyes opened wide, and his mouth fell open in astonishment. "Death penalty?"

"Yes. We have you killing three people. One in Australia and two here."

"Two?"

"Yes, Fausta and Carly."

"Carly? That was an accident. I didn't kill her."

"Oh really? How do you know it was an accident? The case is still under investigation, so nobody knows if it is ruled an accident or not." Roth moved his torso towards Jack. "Only the killer knows if it was an accident or not."

"Admit it Jack, we got you."

"No! You bitch! No!"

Sabine got up. "You came to Florida using a fake passport. You used a fake visa to get a job. You kidnapped your wife, killed her, and buried her body somewhere. And then you killed Carly, making it look like an accident."

"No!"

"Jack, your daughter heard you!" Roth pulled out a photo of Nora and slid it in front of Jack.

"Daughter?" Jack was puzzled. He looked at the photo a bit closer.

"Oh, that's Carly's kid!"

No, Jack. She's your daughter and she heard the whole thing? Oh, and that would qualify as child abuse."

251

"Heard the whole thing? But how..."

Roth hit play on his phone. The first thing that they heard was the infamous phrase and then Sabine was heard asking if it was Jack. They heard Nora confirm it, Sabine asking again, and Nora repeating the confirmation.

"My daughter?" Jack squinted at the photo. Nora was smiling and that smile reminded him of Fausta. "She-she looks just like 'er."

"Yes, Jack, your daughter heard what you did to her mother. Are you proud of that Jack?" Sabine asked.

Jack focused on the photo.

"Jack! Did you kill Fausta?" Roth was determined to break him.

Jack shook his head. "No! No! I didn't kill 'er..." he kept his eyes on Nora. "It was an accident! A horrible accident! I wanted my money is all. I wanted to take her and my money and go back home, where we belonged. Not 'ere! Not in this shithole of a town!" tears were streaming down his cheeks. "I loved Faussy. I didn't know she was expectin'! I would never have allowed her to leave." he said loudly through his tears.

Sid and Terrance looked at each other, smiling.

Both Roth and Sabine sat down. They had accomplished part of their task, but there were more questions.

"Jack, did you kill Carly too?" Roth figured he would play that card while they were on a roll.

"She deserved to die! She deserved to die! She took my Faussy away from me! She had to pay!" he turned to the detectives with pleading eyes, still crying, "Don't you understand? She had to pay for what she did!"

At that point, Roth pulled out one last sheet of paper from the American folder. "Here, sign this and it will all be over." he slid it towards Jack and put a pen on top of it.

Still blubbering, Jack signed it. "Can I see Nora? I need to apologize to 'er."

The two detectives looked at each other, puzzled. Then Roth said: "I'll see what I can do." he placed the signed confession inside the folder, took both folders, and left the room with Sabine. They joined Sid and Terrance in the adjacent room.

"Well, I guess that's it." Roth handed both folders to Terrance.

"Not quite."

"What else do we need, Sid?"

"I need to know where Fausta is buried. We need to give her a proper burial so Nora can have closure."

"Okay, let me see what I can do." Roth went back into the interrogation room, followed by Sabine.

Chapter 19

A small parade of Melbourne and Palm Bay police cruisers, CSI trucks, excavators, fire trucks, a small crane, and the mobile command post were heading toward the Compound. Detective Roth and Sabine were transporting Jack. Terrance and Nora were traveling together. Sid and his son, SJ, were traveling together in a third car driven by Detective Simmons.

"Holy hell, where is this place?" Sid asked Matthew.

"It's called the Compound, and it's in southwest Palm Bay."

"Why would he have brought her all the way there?" SJ asked.

"We don't know exactly, but my guess is that he wanted to bury her body in a secluded place away from suspicious eyes."

"Well, you can't get any more secluded than this godforsaken place!"

SJ nodded as he sat back, trying to relax. "I should have rode with her."

"Be patient, son. You'll be by her side when they find the grave."

"What the hell is wrong with this guy?" SJ couldn't fathom hurting anyone and especially a woman like his fiancée.

"He's sick and evil, son. Unfortunately, there are too many people like him in this world."

"Yeah, SJ, and it's our job to bring these bastards to justice."

As they approached the burial place, the entourage slowed down, and then came to a halt. Detectives Roth and Sabine exited first and gently removed Jack from the back seat. Still in handcuffs and leg irons, Jack walked slowly towards the site which was covered in overgrown hibiscuses and tall grass.

"Right 'ere." he gestured with his head, pointing to the hibiscuses.

Roth waved at the excavation team. "Okay boys, over here."

The heavy equipment leaped into action. They cleared all the overgrown plantation and began the digging process. This had to be done by hand, since they had no idea how deeply the body was buried.

Nora stood at a safe distance with SJ, Sid, and Terrance by her side. She looked over to Jack, noticing his regret while he cried and yelled about how sorry he was, over and over again. Their eyes met a few times. Jack's face was asking for forgiveness, while Nora's face was clearly angry with no sign of forgiveness for this man who killed her mother and auntie.

About twenty minutes in, the offers found a rug that obviously wrapped a body. Both Roth and Sabine approached the burial site, and with a head motion, Roth had the officers unwrap the body. While all this went on, the CSI technicians snapped hundreds upon hundreds of digital photos. Another technician videotaped the entire process. "Okay, let's get her to the medical examiner." then Roth noticed a gold necklace that shining from within the dirt. "Wait. Hey, come over here and take some photos." He put on a rubber glove, and when the CSI walked over, he pulled the necklace. He gently brushed some dirt off and gave it a closer look. He held it for the CSI to photograph. "Huh." he walked over to Nora and handed her the necklace. "Is this hers?"

Nora pouted as tears flowed from her eyes. "Yes...it was a confirmation gift from her parents...she always wore it." Wailing loudly, she dropped to her knees and held the necklace to her bosom. "Oh, Mom! Mommy!" she screamed.

The silence surrounding her was deafening. It showed the emotion that everyone present was feeling. Even Jack was shouting, "I'm sorry! Oh, God, I'm so sorry!" from a good distance away.

"Nora, would you mind giving it to me? We need to enter it into evidence, along with the clothes she's wearing." he extended his hand to her. "We'll give everything back to you once this is over with."

Nora stood up and gave Roth the necklace. Then, drying her eyes with the back of her hand, she slowly walked over to Jack.

Jack stood up to face his daughter. "Oh my God, you're so beautiful. You look so much like her." he cracked a smile under the soot of his tears and the dust that landed on his face.

Nora moved dangerously close to him. "You! You took my mom away from me! How could you? And then you took my auntie Carly! Why? Why?" she stared directly into his eyes.

"I'm sorry! I really am! I loved your mom! I did! Please forgive me, darlin'! I need your forgiveness!"

Nora spat on his face. "I will NEVER forgive you! I hope you rot in hell!" she turned on her heels and walked away.

Everyone's natural impulse was to clap, but they all kept perfectly still as they watched Nora walk back to SJ.

"Can we go now, Uncle Terry?"

"Yes. Let's go."

Nora, SJ, Sid, and Terrance got into one of the cruisers and drove away leaving the rest of the crew there to finish.

~~~~~~

On a typical, beautiful September Florida day, Fausta was laid to rest in a small Catholic Cemetery located on Miller Street in Palm Bay. Gathered around the gravesite were all the people that were involved in Fausta and Carly's investigation: Nora, SJ, Janice, and her grandparents, Vincenzo and Gabriella. Nora sat between her grandparents, not letting go of either. Although it was a bright and sunny day, everyone's tears glistened in the sunshine. As the priest concluded the graveside service, the guests found closure in their own way. After the ceremony, Nora approached her mother's coffin and gently threw the pink rose on it.

"Addio figlia mia," Gabriella exclaimed through her tears as she threw her rose on top of her daughter's coffin.

"Vai con Dio, figlia mia." Vincenzo threw his rose, pulled out his handkerchief, and wiped his tears.

One by one, all the guests did the same. After the burial, all gathered inside the tiny church for a small reception.

Roth approached Nora and opened his arms. She gave him a warm hug.

"Thanks for coming, detective."

"I wouldn't have missed it." he pulled a small box from his jacket pocket. "Here, this belongs to you."

Nora took the small box and opened it. Fausta's gold necklace shimmered inside. "It looks like new."

"I had it cleaned just for you."

She hugged him again. "Thank you for everything, detective."

"Don't mention it."

After every last guest had left, Nora walked over to the grave. "Just give me a moment, please?" she asked her grandparents.

They nodded while embracing each other.

She stood silent while collecting her thoughts. "Mommy, you were right, and I didn't listen to you. I'm sorry Mommy." tears formed again. "But you're with Auntie Carly now and I know you're gonna have a blast up there." She smiled faintly. "And Auntie Carly, take care of my Mommy, okay? I love you both so very much and I'm gonna miss you SO much." then she looked up to the clear blue sky. "God, you took them from me so early, so you better take care of them. Promise me?" she made the sign of the cross and slowly walked away.

~~~~~~

"Are you ready, Honeybun?" Terrance looked into the eyes of the most beautiful bride he'd ever seen.

"Yes, Uncle Terry, I'm ready." she hooked her left arm into Terrance's and they both slowly began walking down the aisle.

The Twin Palms Hotel had decorated the beach with an arch festooned with hibiscus flowers and seashells. About a dozen chairs were decorated with white organza tied in huge bows in the back. A three-piece band made up of a violin, a bass, and a flute played the Wedding March, with the breaking waves providing tempo. The guests stood, admiring in awe, the beauty and elegance of the bride walking down the aisle.

Her grandparents proudly waved and blew her kisses as they admired their only granddaughter wearing Fausta's wedding dress. When they found out about the upcoming Christmas wedding, Gabriella had taken it upon herself to search for and alter Fausta's wedding dress. The finished product was incredible, and this "something old" looked just as perfect on Nora as it had on Fausta.

The Welbys were also present. April brought the garter she wore when she married Kevin. Obviously, it didn't show under the beautiful gown, but April knew the "something borrowed" would bestow good luck on this marriage, just as it did on their own.

Janice had the honor of giving Nora the "something blue," a gold brooch with a blue sapphire set in the center. Nora had it on the right side of her gown, just above her breast. It had been given to her by Sid's mother on her wedding day, so she knew of no better woman to have it than the woman who loved her son almost as much as she did. She blew a kiss to her soon-to-be daughter-in-law.

The "something new"? That was going to be her new life with SJ that was to begin very shortly. As she passed, each person tried to get her attention by waving or nodding their heads, but Nora's attention was directed at her groom, who had been by her side throughout the entire ordeal. He was steadfast, never wavering. He was there only for her, and he continued to love her with all of his might.

After the minister declared that the two were husband and wife he said: "You may kiss your bride."

SJ and Nora kissed passionately and sensually. Then SJ dipped his new wife, until she almost hit the sand. "I love you Nora, with all of me."

The new gushing bride looked right into her new husband's eyes and said: "I love you SJ, with all of me, too."

SJ lifted his wife, and hand-in-hand, they ran down the sandy aisle while the entourage cheered and clapped.

As the guests entered the dining room, one of Janice's cousins from New York approached the bride and groom's table.

"Oh, hello, Uncle Tony, I'm so glad you could make it." SJ exclaimed.

"Yeah, kid, sorry I'm late. Our plane took off almost an hour late from JFK and we didn't get into Mel-born until six."

The bride and groom burst out laughing.

"What's so funny?" Tony smirked.

"It's Mel-burn, Uncle Tony, not Mel-born."

"Yeah, yeah, I'm from New York so..."

THE END

As an indie…

…(**independent**) author I rely on reviews. In fact, those gold stars are indie authors' lifelines. If you truly care about your favorite indie author, please leave a review on at least one of the following websites:

Amazon - www.amazon.com

Barnes & Noble - www.BarnesandNoble.com

BookBub- www.BookBub.com

Goodreads - www.goodreads.com

Google Books - https://play.google.com

iBooks App - https://iBooks.com

Thank you so much for your support. Don't forget, I write for you!

Your favorite author,

Joanne Fisher

And now, please enjoy a small excerpt of my next novella from my *Christmas In...* series, *Christmas in Rome*.

Carlotta was waiting anxiously for Matthew to arrive. She held a sign that read **Matthew Ruffolo**. She waved the sign in the air with every man that met the description of the photo she had in her possession. Finally, the real Matthew exited the sterile area. Noticing the sign Penelope was holding, he waved in her direction. He was much better looking in person than in the photo, with dirty blonde hair, emerald-green eyes, and a slim but muscular build. Standing at over six feet, he towered over her when they approached each other.

Wow, he thought as he smiled at her. She wasn't very tall, but she was an Italian beauty with deep dark eyes, wavy obsidian hair, and a figure that was the epitome of a fifties-era Italian actress.

"Mateu?" she asked with a sensual Italian accent.

Amused by her accent, he just couldn't correct her. "Yes, and you must be Carlotta?"

"Yes, very nice to meet you."

At that moment, as they shook hands, a spark of electricity passed between them.

"Where's Agatella?"

"Oh, she's at home. She doesn't know about the situation yet."

"Oh? Isn't that a bit unethical?"

"Perhaps, but I feel I must get to know the father before I allow the meeting."

"All right, I can respect that."

"Good. Come, let's go."

"Gladly."

Together, they zigzagged out of the airport. Knowing that Carlotta was leading him to her car, he followed her like a new puppy. *I like this woman.*

"Have you ever been to Rome?"

"No, this will be my first time."

"Meraviglioso! You're going to love the Eternal City! I promise!"

"I have no doubt."

"Here we are." She stopped by a silver FIAT 500.

Matthew gave her a perplexed look. "Um, I don't think I'm going to fit in there."

"Oh, come on, you Americans and your big things."

He had the perfect rebuttal but decided to keep it to himself since he barely knew the woman and didn't want to get off on the wrong foot.

She opened the trunk, and amazingly, his large duffle bag fit in nicely. He kept his carry-on with his computer with him. He opened the driver door and waited until she was comfortably seated and then he gently shut it. He whizzed around to the other side.

"Okay, here goes." He opened his door, sat in the seat, adjusted the seat, buckled his seat belt, placed his computer bag on his lap, and gave Carlotta a big smile. "Okay, so you were right. Let's go!"

Made in the USA
Middletown, DE
28 April 2022

64835229R00168